RIDE THE HIGH HILLS

When Grandpaw Toween was killed in a raid on his ranchhouse by the landgrabbing Tollers, Will Dayton felt he had to help the old man's granddaughter, Minty, get her cows to Warbonnet to raise money to pay off the mortgage. There was the herd to gather and one hundred miles to travel. For crew, he had two men and a girl, with just one horse each... Dayton hadn't wanted any part of the Toween troubles, and he wasn't interested in Minty – at first – but a man couldn't just leave a girl in a situation like that.

RIDE THE HIGH HILLS

RIDE THE HIGH HILLS

by

Dave Waldo

Dales Large Print Books
Long Preston, North Yorkshire,
BD23 4ND, England.

British Library Cataloguing in Publication Data.

Waldo, Dave
    Ride the high hills.

    A catalogue record of this book is
    available from the British Library

    ISBN   1-84262-394-X pbk

First published in Great Britain in 1963
by Ward Lock and Company Limited

Published in Large Print 2005 by arrangement with
Dave Waldo, care of Rupert Crew Limited

Dales Large Print is an imprint of Library Magna Books Ltd.

Printed and bound in Great Britain by
T.J. (International) Ltd., Cornwall, PL28 8RW

TO GWEN

CHAPTER ONE

Standing there in the Omaha cemetery a stranger among strangers in the cold wet April afternoon Dayton was aware of only one urgent need. To be done with it all, with the mumbled ceremonial, the meaningless words, the moist hand-clasps of unknown folks, unsmiling as befitted the occasion, only their eyes showing the high shine of curiosity about him. Amy's relatives and friends, some from Omaha, some from farther East, all here for her funeral and all looking at the stranger who had carried Amy off into the great American desert.

Sombrely he stared at the earth, half-hearing the voice of the preacher and then with sudden pain the irrevocable words:

'Ashes to ashes, dust to dust.'

He turned away then unable to endure more, made his way, unseeing, through the little circle of black-clad mourners. Someone touched his arm but he strode on, out of the cemetery and through the outlying quarters of the growing town to the railroad station. Here in 1876 a big U.P depot was now in full operation. Here he waited for a train that would take him back where he belonged, to the frontier and the open range of the Territory. He stood then in the late afternoon on the West-bound departure platform among the drummers, miners, labourers and others more profitably occupied, he figured, in land deals, gambling and honky-tonks. He knew them all, had met their kind on the cattle trails from southern Texas, in the boom towns running with the railroad from Nebraska to California, in the tough frontier towns in which he'd fought in his hard uncompromising way for the rights and profits of the U.P railroad. He assessed them coldly and unsmilingly, aware of their capacity for endurance, their occasional courage, their moments of fear, their follies and treacheries.

The train came jangling and puffing in and Dayton climbed aboard, found himself an inner seat, put his carpet bag on the rack and composed himself for the fifteen hours run that lay between him and Bridgerville. The train got under way to a chorus of whistles and shouts. He slouched deeper in his seat, trying to shut out everything, or almost everything. He could never shut out the bitter run of his personal thoughts.

The conductor came along the centre aisle and looking down, saw him. 'Well, if it isn't Mr Dayton,' he said, 'We sure don't see you often in these parts.' He paused and leaned over the seat. 'What brings you so far East?'

'Family affairs,' said Dayton softly.

'Don't see you as a family man,' said the conductor, bluntly. He went on staring down at the big man in his seat. 'Still I guess it's all of two years since you was workin' on the bridge over Smoky River. Come to think of it, a whole lot of water's passed under that bridge since you ram-rodded the crew that built it. An' a lot can happen in two years. Yessir.'

'Yes,' said Dayton coldly. The conductor stared at him a moment's space with the curiosity of a sociable man. Then he shrugged.

'Be seein' you again, Mr Dayton.' He walked on down the swaying length of the car. Yes, thought Dayton, a lot can happen, a lot has happened. A whole new life begun and then ended almost as soon as it had begun. And it had not even begun properly – not in Bridgerville, not among the saloons and red-lights, the cursing, brawling freighters and the tough miners and the half-wild cowhands. A man after marriage began to see through his wife's eyes as well as his own. What in his bachelor days he had accepted as normal had after a month of marriage begun to look suddenly new and strange. He had nothing against punchers in town to see the tiger or miners carousing in the saloons. It was the life of the frontier, to be found in every new and raw community in the West, but marriage put him apart from it. Above all Amy had hated it and nothing that he could say reconciled her to what she had called 'these barbarians'. He had wondered sometimes why she had chosen to marry him. After all he was one of them. And then she had begun to complain of pain and exhaustion and at last he had sent her home to Omaha and then she had died, fortunately perhaps, he thought, staring now out of the vast shadow of night coming down over the Nebraska prairie, fortunately perhaps among the people she knew and understood. The sombre pain that her death had awakened was still alive in him. Maybe it would always be alive, together with the profound sense of failure that went with it.

Two men in brown derbies and high-buttoned store clothes came seeking players for a poker game. Dayton watched their slow sociable progress down the car, the easy

12

smiles, the special look for the two Cyprians sitting just ahead of him. He refused their offer of a game gently and they did not press it. Eventually they found enough to sit in and returned to their own car. An attendant lit the big brass lamps and went away. Dayton fell into a doze and then into a deep sleep. He woke occasionally and irritably, to shift a little on the hard seat. And like this the long hours passed until waking again he saw the first faint grey of dawn magically changing the unseen world into dim black shapes of rocks and trees or a solitary cabin in the vast empty prairie.

He went out and stood unsteadily on the observation platform of the last car. The train lurched and swayed through the dark Wyoming night, steadily eating up the last of the long miles between Omaha and Bridgerville. He had a carpet bag in his left hand. Not more than ten miles to Bridgerville and not a friend in the whole place. He opened the bag and felt under the shirts and underwear for a familiar shape. He pulled it out, a holstered gun and belt. He put the bag down and strapped the belt around his waist. It was there and the feel of the smooth walnut butt was reassuring. For two weeks in Omaha he had not worn it out of deference to the occasion; but he had felt lost without it. Over the long hard years of cattle-driving and ramrodding the construction gang it had become a part of him.

Marshal Merlees said, 'Don't come back, Will. There's nothin' but grief an' trouble for you in this place.' But after Amy's funeral there was nowhere to go but Bridgerville. Boom-camp, railroad hell on wheels, man's sprawling obscenity on the dignity of the desert, it was still the only place he knew and anyway he was double-damned if they were going to tell him where to go and where not to go.

The bell way ahead clanged twice and the train slowed down for a signal. Then it picked up again and began to rumble over the bridge spanning Cheyenne Wash. He remembered the place with something almost of affection as a man remembered with a kind of love other places in which he had toiled and suffered and fought. It had been hell to build but they'd done it with the same warming zest that had built the rest of the line. And now that was all over and he was going back to the saloons, the honky-tonks, and the dark alleys, to the Tollers who ruled their range and the town, to the shop-keepers and citizens who paid lip-service to

14

law and order, to all the folk who hated his guts. They'd know he was coming. And they'd be waiting for the first sign of weakness, for the first chance to get back at him, the bully boys he'd whipped into line, the workers he'd sacked, the brothel-keepers and the women, above all the Tollers, against whom he'd fought a one-man war in the interests of the railroad.

The train bell jangled again up front. That meant no more than a half-mile from town. He waited and tension knotted his stomach muscles. His hand moved once more to the holstered gun. But it was loose, waiting as so often before to come to his aid, to flame and roar into deathly life.

The brakes began to come on and now he could see the sheds and shanties outside the station. He gripped the bag, making ready to leave the train as unobtrusively as possible. Slowly the engine and five cars ground to a standstill. There was a great hissing of steam and some indistinct shouting from the direction of the engine. Dayton swung his legs over the rail of the platform and slid down onto the track. He stood for a moment breathing in the wild heady scents of the spring morning. He shook his head as if to clear it and then cat-footed his way towards

15

the cover of the depot buildings.

There were two figures standing indistinctly against the background of steam and smoke outside the agent's office. Dayton went on around the dark back of the grain store and so reached the street. It led through a cottonwood grove to the town's main intersection with the two big false-fronted saloons, the Drovers Hotel and the Diamond.

He walked on keeping in the shadow of the big trees. In three minutes he reached the board-walk outside the Drovers and, as people swung and stared, losing their thread of gossip, he climbed the steps and crossing the porch without looking either left or right made his way indoors.

Zack Trant, the desk clerk, paled as the tall figure of Dayton crossed the foyer. He fiddled with the register, coughed self-consciously and waited.

Dayton stopped at the desk.

'I'll have the key of my room, Zack,' he said.

Trant looked up at Dayton, his eyes troubled, his breathing fast.

'You shouldn't have come back, Mr Dayton,' he said. 'You just shouldn't have come.'

'Reckon my comings and goings are

16

mainly my affair, son,' he said patiently. 'Let's have the key.'

The clerk reached for the key and handed it silently across the desk. 'The Tollers are in town, Mr Dayton,' he said as Dayton picked it up. 'So?' said Dayton.

'They're waitin' a chance to gun you down. They ain't never forgot the way you bulled the railroad across their range.' Dayton turned away.

'They can sure have a try, son,' he said, over his shoulder. 'There's nothing to stop anyone from having a try.'

He went upstairs to the room they'd lived in for that short nine months. He stood in the doorway looking at it. At the frilled lace curtains that had mocked Amy's efforts to ignore the town's raw brutality, at the dressing table where she had sat so often staring hopelessly at her reflection in the glass, at the velvet drapes and the picture called 'Cherry Ripe' over the mantelpiece, a picture neither of them had liked overmuch. The room now looked like just what it was, a hotel bedroom in a frontier town. Dolled up with the curtains, the mirror and the picture but as impersonal and empty as a room could be. And it was this he couldn't face, not now. Not any more emptiness to

17

add to the emptiness within him.

He dumped his carpet bag on the bed. Undressing down to his underwear, he went to the wash-stand and shaved and washed in cold water from the rose-patterned ewer. He put on a clean shirt, combed his long brown hair. He put on some grey woollen working pants, tucking the ends into his high-heeled black Californian boots. He would keep his gun and belt with him. He drew the gun, broke it, examined the mechanism and re-loaded it. He thrust it back in its holster. He knotted a blue scarf round the brown column of his throat and pulled on the leather vest and old cord jacket he had worn for years.

He'd have his meal and his drink at the bar and then he'd go. Go where? The words echoed in his head as he closed the door of the bedroom behind him and went on echoing dismally as he walked down to the long bar. He made his way through the card-tables towards the bar. Talk seemed to die away as men saw him. Greener Pete the barman was up at the far end in low-toned conversation with a couple of customers. Dayton remembered them on the train. City clothes and Derby hats. Drummers with smooth manners and a never-ending thirst for orders and samples of their own whisky and cigars.

The group turned to look at him as he stood there waiting for Pete to serve him. At something said one of the drummers gave a high-pitched cackling laugh. Dayton looked at his own tall reflection in the back-bar mirror, at the neat rows of bottles, at the advertising cards, at the medium sized oleograph of a wild-looking long-haired ranny on a rearing horse with the words below, 'Pony Express'. Some Eastern artist's impossible idea of what went on in 1860.

And then Pete came into his line of vision and was saying: 'Howdy, Mr Dayton.'

Dayton said, 'Howdy! Same as usual, Pete.'

The barman put a shot glass and bottle in front of him. 'They was askin' how come I'm called Greener,' he said as if explaining the laughter. 'I told them about the double-bar'l I've got under the bar. They seemed to think it was kinda funny.'

'They wouldn't have a year ago when Big-Nose George tried to hold the place up,' said Dayton, reaching for the bottle. He poured the shot-glass half-full and downed the whisky in one. Greener Pete watched him uneasily.

'You fixin' to stay long, Mr Dayton?'

'Mebbe.'

'Ain't a worthwhile town any longer,' said the barman. 'Now the railroad's done there's only the Tollers and their crew of hard-cases.'

'I don't aim to be hurried,' said Dayton.

'They're a big-mouthed bunch,' said the barman reassuringly.

There was a noise from the entrance to the saloon and looking in the wide mirror behind the bar, Dayton saw the batwing doors slap open and a group of men swagger in. He recognised them immediately. The Toller crew with their ramrod Jed Moss bulking large at their head. They saw him and momentarily paused. Then Moss said something and they crowded forward again towards the bar making a small noisy knot between Dayton and the two drummers.

For a time they ignored him, preferring to aim their talk at the two drummers, drinking swiftly, laughing over-loud. Then as Dayton raised his shot-glass to his lips for a second time, he was aware of a sudden stop in the noise. A gun roared suddenly and the bottle in front of him was shattered into fragments. Its contents splashed on the bar-top and over his vest.

20

Dayton placed his glass in the puddle of whisky and turned slowly to face the T-Bar hands. He was aware as he did so of the absolute silence in the long bar-room, of Pete tense over the other side of the bar, of the five faces watching him with a kind of nervous mockery as his eyes met theirs.

'Which of you did it?' The words came at last, slowly and deliberately. 'Ask Pete,' said Moss, with a measured and deliberate insolence. He was almost off-guard for a split second but did not fall into the trap. Instead he began to walk up the length of the bar towards them.

'Don't come any further, Dayton,' Moss said abruptly when the tall man was five yards from him.

Dayton made no reply. He walked on. His Colt was suddenly in his right hand and someone at the card-tables gasped audibly. His eyes hard and unwavering bored into Moss's. 'I asked you a question,' he said. 'I'm waiting your answer.' Moss laughed, a hard jarring sound in the quiet room.

'There ain't any answer, Dayton. You've sung your song. Now mosey on.'

'Not before you've paid for another bottle of whisky,' said Dayton.

'The hell with you,' came the foreman's

21

answer. He saw the muzzle of Dayton's big Colt rise a fraction of an inch and fear pulled at the muscles around his mouth and his eyes wavered unsteadily. 'You wouldn't shoot a man without giving him a chance to draw.' The words came out in a dry whisper of fear and uncertainty.

'No,' said Dayton, 'I wouldn't,' and then he brought the gun up and hard down on the man's temple. The foreman crumpled at the feet of his men. They stood staring down at him as if at a loss. 'Pack him out of here,' said Dayton.

Slowly the T-Bar hands picked up Moss and carrying the sprawling unconscious figure made their way out of the saloon.

CHAPTER TWO

Dayton watched the Tollers leave and then turned to the barman. 'Give me another bottle, Greener,' he said, 'And charge both to me.'

The barman produced a second bottle. 'Better have yourself a good long drink before someone else comes bustin' in, Mr Dayton.'

'Yes,' said Dayton and refilled his shot-glass. He drank the whisky slowly and appreciatively. Then he refilled the glass. Before touching it he dug into his vest pocket and produced a sack of tobacco and papers. Deftly he rolled himself a cigarette, lit it and smoked it slowly with his second drink.

Greener Pete wiped a glass with a cloth.

'The Toween note falls due in just over a week,' he said.

'Toween?'

'Yeah, sure. He borrowed from the Bank a coupla years back to restock. Got a small ranch north of the Tollers range, only place with real water on it. The Tollers bought the note from the Bank. Reckon there'll be trouble up there. Old Toween ain't goin' to like bein' herded off his land.'

'If the Tollers hold the note then he'll have to quit,' Dayton said. 'That's the law.' He raised his glass to drink again and paused with the glass half-way to his lips as a fusillade of shots rang out in the street. It was followed by the high panicky whinnying of a scared horse and then above it all a woman's shrill cry of fear. Dayton turned and ran to the door. Outside the whole story was before him clear in the bright sunlight. A flat-bed wagon stood in the centre of the street, a small figure erect on the driving seat. The two horses were rearing up, pawing the air, about to bolt. She was trying to fight them down with reins and whip. Dayton ran out, grabbed the nearest horse's mane and pulled it down. He held on with all his strength, fought the big bay down until both horses stood trembling and frothing and the danger was past.

'Thanks, mister,' said a voice from the wagon and he squinted up at her through the glaring light.

'What scared them?'

'The Toller crew,' she said bitterly.

'They're mighty good at scaring horses an' women.'

He took a good look at her while she was speaking. She was a small well-rounded girl with short tousled hair, almost like a boy, in her tight jeans and clipped speech.

'You all right, Miz Toween?' said a voice and turning Dayton saw it was Sam Merlees, the marshal. 'I was way down street when it happened an' too far off to lend a hand.' He turned to Dayton. 'Howdy, Will!'

'Howdy, Sam!' said Dayton.

'You didn't oughter ride in here alone, Miz Toween. The Tollers got no love fer you or your grandpa.'

'I'll ride in when it suits me, Sam Merlees,' she said levelly. 'An' if I didn't ride in what d'you figure we're goin' to live on – grass and water like the cattle?'

'You won't have the water long. The note's due in ten days' time.'

'We'll see. We'll see. We ain't beat yet.' She stood up shaking out the reins with a quick angry movement. Then she seemed to remember Dayton and she looked down at him.

'Thanks again, Mister,' she said.

'Will Dayton,' she said.

She flicked the horses then and moved off

down street. The two men watched the wagon roll away.

'Reckon you've about reached the end of your rope, Will,' the marshal said, softly. Will Dayton looked at the tall figure on the broadwalk. 'Yeah,' he said at last. 'Reckon I have.'

'You'll be doing me an' the other folks in this town a favour if you'd ride on jest as soon as you can, Will. There ain't no welcome for you in this town – not any more. If the Tollers thought we were sidin' you, they'd pull the place to pieces.'

He stood there, but the words sank in, reminding him only of what he had known for weeks. He had lost everything since Amy died, his job, his friends.

'I'll ride,' he said. 'I'll ride on now.'

He began to walk across the street towards the Mason House where he had a room. The marshal followed him.

'You want any help, Will? I'll stake if need be,' he said. Dayton made no answer. Some faint hope had buoyed him up, some vague intention to settle down in Bridgerville. But now he knew it was too late. He didn't want Sam Merlees' help. He didn't want anything except to collect the few possibles that remained.

Slowly he climbed the stairs of the Mason House, lurching a little through the door of his room. He stood there for a moment. He slowly, awkwardly pulled two saddle-bags from under the bed. Moving like a man in a dream he stuffed shirts and underwear into them. From the wash stand he fetched a razor, brush and soap which he wrapped in a half-sheet of newspaper. Something made him turn towards the door. Sam Merlees, stood there, his eyes sad and speculative.

'You don't have to stand there and watch every move I make, Sam. I told you I'd ride on,' he said, irritably.

'Yeah, I know,' said Merlees. 'Figured I might be able to lend you a hand. Ain't never had nothing agin you, Will.' He leaned against the door, a tall lean hard man, with the long years of thankless duty behind him, gunfights and fist-fights, trail-hands maddened with the red-eye whisky and the soiled doves who rode the circuit of the new railroads, the boom camp and the trail towns. Will Dayton stood there staring at the marshal. Nothing showed. Sam Merlees remained untouched by the dirt he lived with. 'Where you aimin' to go, Will?'

Dayton pulled a gunbelt and holstered six gun out of a drawer and strapped them on around his lean waist. He ignored the question.

'It's a mighty big country,' continued Merlees, unaffected by Dayton's silence. 'Nothin' a man can't do, if he's prepared to work. This territory's almost virgin land. Almost wish I was a young man again. I'd enjoy fightin' the land an' beatin' it.'

Dayton lifted his saddle-bags, settled a broad-brimmed Stetson on his head and picking up a Winchester that stood in the corner next the door shouldered his way past Merlees. The marshal followed him imperturbably downstairs and out into the street.

They made their way diagonally across the street. The mud was beginning to steam in the sudden heat of the late April sun. The Marshal remained a step behind Dayton, his normally long face made even longer and sadder by Dayton's complete rejection of every advance. The livery stable was the last house but one in Main Street. It stood out trim and freshly painted since Mark Toller had taken it over and installed Whitey Loomis as the hostler.

Dayton walked in to the cool darkness of the stable. Whitey Loomis limped towards them.

'You can saddle up the bay,' Dayton said abruptly.

Loomis looked as if it would be worth talking about. His small pale eyes shifted from Dayton to the marshal and speculatively back to Dayton.

'You aimin' to ride on?'

'That's it,' said Dayton.

Loomis wilted a little under their combined coldness. He turned away and lifted a saddle down off the rack. He hefted it into a stall and saddled up Dayton's horse.

Dayton watched every move of the hostler, aware of Merlees lounging against the door jamb but determined to say no more. Loomis led the bay out into the stable entrance. The horse was sleek and well-cared for. Dayton paid his bill and walked the horse out into the sunlight. Merlees and Loomis watched him from the doorway of the stable. He climbed heavily in the saddle felt the bay's one moment of tension and then without another word he headed it out of town.

The north trail led across a stretch of arid desert towards a range of low hills. Idly Dayton noted the fresh tracks of a wagon and two horses. That would belong to the girl. He rode on, feeling only a slow smouldering anger with everything, but most of all with himself. The spur line from White Rock had been completed a month ago and since then his whole life seemed to have changed.

There had been nothing to think of when the job was done. Amy had died in Omaha, visiting her folks, escaping from the monotony of life in a railroad camp. He had buried his grief out on the prairie, alone with the coyote and the buzzard-hawk. He had nursed the railway through the hazards of construction to its last day of completion when Indian raids, rock falls, blizzards and howling winds no longer mattered except as vague shadows in the beat-up past.

Slowly he rode up to the crest of the first hill, pausing there for a brief survey of the surrounding country. It was a part of him now, this unhurried contemplation of what lay ahead. Staring out across the flat stretch of desert he saw a small ball of dust roll down out of the distant hill-country. A rider from Mark Toller's spread on his way to town. Mark Toller himself, perhaps, on his big black, counting his acres or his cattle. Who cared? He put the bay gently down the long slope. Only one thing was troublesome and that was a sudden craving for a drink. 'Just one drink, horse,' he said aloud.

The bay pricked up its ears as if interested. But then horses don't have to bother. No wonder folks talked of horse-sense. No horse mucked up its life swallowing firewater. For why? To forget. Forget Amy. Forget the war, forget the job you did well, forget yourself.

They reached a valley circling through hill country about an hour later. The sun rode high above them. Time to make camp and eat, thought Dayton. And then clear and hard, splitting the fine quiet of early afternoon there came three gunshots, with about three seconds between each of them.

Dayton reined in, halted, listened. The shots seemed to have come from behind the out-jutting shoulder of hill that hid the far end of the valley. There was a fourth shot and then almost in its echo he thought he heard a high cry, a woman's scream.

He touched the bay with his spurs and rode towards the noise. He rounded the bend in the valley. Right in the middle stood a flat-bed wagon and team of horses. A little way off two horses, a clay-bank and a buckskin, grazed. Near the wagon a girl was struggling in a man's arms. The man looked big enough but he had both hands full. Close by a second man stood and laughed.

Dayton rode up to the little group. He sat his horse looking down at them. The man holding the struggling, kicking girl, aware of a new arrival, relaxed his grip. The girl jerked herself free but not without tearing her shirt, a grey boyish shirt. There was nothing boyish about her bare breast showing whitely through the torn shirt. Dayton remembered her then. The girl who had been in town with the wagon. She stood back against the wagon, her breast heaving. There were tears in her eyes and vainly she sought to repair the damage done to her shirt.

Dayton looked at the man who had been holding her. It was Brad Toller.

'What goes on?' he asked mildly.

The big man's eyes were wild, there was a pallor around his mouth and a nerve twitched in his right temple.

'No concern of yours,' he said jerkily.

'When I see a young girl being wrestled like a bear I figure it is my concern,' said Dayton, his tone still mild.

The girl's assailant glared at him and then as Dayton eyed him, very grudgingly he said:

'She's trespassing, Mister Dayton, just to satisfy your all-fired curiosity. This is T-Bar range. She's got no right to be on it. An' for that matter neither have you.'

'Don't see any reason to muss her up for a mite of trespassing,' observed Dayton. 'Maybe she lost her way.'

'Lost her way. Why she belongs to that goddam nester, Toween.'

'I don't belong to nobody,' the girl suddenly interrupted. 'John Toween is my grandpaw. An' these two men fired at me until I pulled in. Then that one' – she pointed at her assailant – 'Brad Toller, who thinks he owns the earth as well as the T-Bar, grabbed me. He said … he said…' Anger or maybe something deeper choked off the words.

'What did he say, girl?' said Dayton gently.

She stared at him for a moment. Then–

'He said I could pay him off for trespassing in kisses. I wouldn't let him touch me in a million years.'

Dayton watched her thoughtfully for a long moment. Small, slightly grimy, with superbly rounded limbs, too dangerously revealed by the skin-tight levis she wore. A child, he thought, unaware that she was now a woman and an invitation in all her ignorance to lobo wolves like Toller and his fellow rider. Unaware of his frank appraisal he saw the colour mount hotly into her cheeks and quickly he turned his questioning eye towards Toller.

'She's a goddam little liar,' said Toller sullenly.

'Reckon you could ride on now,' said Dayton. 'I'll see the girl on her way.'

'Ride on! Ride on! Just like that.' Toller turned to the other rider. 'You hear that, Sam? Ride on. Over my own land.' He turned again to Dayton. 'Get off that goddam horse, mister, and I'll show you who's goin' to ride on.'

Dayton dismounted leisurely. He led the bay to the wagon and tied the reins to a wheel spoke. Then he took off his gun belt and holster. He removed the gun and handed it to the girl.

'If I don't come off best,' he said, 'and there's any more hanky-panky use this on them.'

Then he turned towards Toller.

'Now,' he said. 'Let's get down to cases, mister.'

Dayton moved in on his opponent at once, swinging a hard right to the man's ribs and following up with a left that almost knocked Toller off balance. Toller was a big man, however, and he bore in now with a sledge-hammer punch that landed on Dayton's temple. It rocked him and before he could recover Toller charged into him and knocked him over. The big cattleman followed up with a swinging kick at Dayton's ribs but Dayton rolled away and Toller, off balance, fell heavily. Dayton climbed to his feet, his breathing fast and unsteady. Toller charged into him, fists pounding. Dayton beat him off. They circled, waiting for an opening.

'Kick his teeth in, Brad,' said the man called Sam.

'Keep out of it, mister.' The girl waggled the gun she was holding.

Toller came in and swung a long right at Dayton's jaw. Dayton ducked and came up with both hands at the now wide-open Toller. He hit him twice in the midriff and then with a vicious uppercut to the jaw almost lifted him off his feet. Toller fell heavily and lay still.

Dayton stood staring down at his opponent. He swayed a little as he stood breathing with great difficulty. Then he turned towards the other man.

'You want in on this?' he said thickly.

'No, sir,' said the other promptly. 'I'll just pack the boss on his cayuse an' git goin'.'

The figure at Dayton's feet began to move, slowly and painfully. There was blood around Toller's mouth but his eyes were still wild with rage in spite of the beating he had taken.

He got to his feet at last, the others watching with the silence always accorded to a defeated man. Then he walked hesitantly over to his horse and climbed heavily into the saddle. He sat there for a moment, unspeaking, although his mouth worked with rage. Then he growled out, 'I'll make you an' the girl and her grandpa pay for this if it's the last thing I ever do.'

Swaying a little in the saddle Brad Toller rode away accompanied by his friend, Sam. Dayton and the girl watched them go.

'They're pretty big folk around here,' she said. There was a moment's pause and looking at her he saw the small frown on her forehead.

'They got enough land without taking from folks like you,' he said.

'My grandpaw's spread's the best small one for miles around, mister. An' what's more he's got the best waterin' for his cattle too. Their streams dry up always by mid-June. But they'll take it like they've taken everything else they've wanted.'

She turned away without waiting for the question that he was about to ask, and clambered up onto the wagon. Dayton whistled up his horse, climbed into the saddle and as the girl whipped up the horses, he began to ride parallel with her.

When they had travelled in silence the length of the valley he put his question. 'How can the Tollers take your grandpa's spread away from him?' Without looking at him she shouted, 'They kin burn us out or shoot us out. They could hang my grandpaw an' say it was fer rustlin'. But they won't do none of these things.'

The wagon lurched heavily over uneven ground and there was silence as she fought the horses into a smoother run.

'No,' she shouted again. 'They'll jest do it legal-like. Grandpaw owes the bank four thousand dollars. His note falls due in ten more days. If he can't meet his debt, the bank'll take over his land. Toller owns the bank like everything else.'

'Why don't your grandpaw sell his cattle – that is, if he's got any?'

'He's got over three hundred head but you can't sell cattle unless you take 'em to market, and we cain't git them to market, mister.'

'Why not?'

'Because the Tollers bought up two of our hands a week ago and even if we tried to git them to Warbonnet they'd stampede 'em on the way.'

The girl put the wagon hard at an unsloping track which led over a ridge. She paused on the spine of the hill and pointed ahead.

'That's grandpaw's range,' she said.

They were deeper now into the hill country. A long valley hemmed in by the hills stretched before them for about eight miles, Dayton guessed, to the base of the high ground. In the last bright light of afternoon it lay before them tranquil and richly green. There were small brown knots of cattle grazing and what looked like a ranch about midway up the valley.

'That's it,' said the girl quietly. 'An' I love it more than anything else in the world.'

Dayton grunted and putting spurs to the bay began to lead the way down to level ground.

CHAPTER THREE

It took them over an hour to reach the
Toween ranch. The trail led through rich
heavy buffalo grass. Occasionally they
passed a heap of whitening bones.

''Tis said the buffalo used to graze here.
Thousands of buffalo, so thick, Grandpaw
says, the whole valley floor was brown. He
saw that twenty years ago when he first rid
thru' here.'

'I've seen 'em,' said Dayton. 'Mighty
peaceful like and grazing one minute and
then the next on the run. So many of 'em it
felt like an earthquake.'

In memory he was back five years or more.
A man found it hard to count the passing
years. And five years at least had passed
since he had last crossed the Missouri and
come out on the Kansas plains. He had
come through them that time with a wagon
train making north and there on the
limitless prairies they had met the buffalo.

'An old trapper I met in Cheyenne once
told me there were over a hundred million

buffalo on the plains in 1860. It ain't like that any more. Maybe it's a pity.'

'Buffalo,' said the girl, 'is a heap more human than a lot of humans I've met with.'

'Could be,' said Dayton and wondered why he was riding along like this talking to a girl he didn't know about animals he wasn't interested in anyways.

'Here's home,' said the girl as they topped one more small rise. Dayton stared at the squat run-down ranch house before them. A minute human habitation against the wilderness backdrop of the Watanope Range. It had been built a good many years back of split pine logs, now weathered to a uniform grey. It had two shuttered windows and a door, outside which stood a barrel and a dipper hanging on a nail. Left of the house was a fair-sized corral, its fence-posts sagging, wire trailing. There was a small bunkhouse. Two horses raised suspicious heads as they drew near. As they reined in a dog ran out barking to greet them. The girl called out, 'Down there, Soppy,' and the dog subsided, growling a little. She got down from the wagon.

'You'd be welcome to eat here, mister, if you've a mind,' she said, looking up at Dayton.

He fiddled with the reins, aware of her scrutiny, aware too that he hadn't figured on getting mixed up with folks. He wanted only to ride on.

A man limped out onto the porch. He was short, square, white-haired. 'You're tarnation slow in gittin' back, Minty,' he called out. Then his eyes seemed to focus on Dayton. 'Who's the young fellow a-sittin' his horse like some pie-eyed statue?'

'Don't rightly know, grandpaw,' said the girl now busy unhitching her team. 'All I know is he gave Brad Toller a beatin' for tryin' to kiss me.'

'Why that good-fer-nothin' son,' said the old man. 'I'll cut him down to size with my shot-gun when I see him.' He advanced towards Dayton, hobbling as he came. 'Light and rest, stranger. Anyone is kind to my Minty is right welcome in my house.'

Dayton slowly swung himself down from the bay. The old man held out a bony hand.

'I'm John Toween, stranger.'

'Will Dayton.' Grasping the old man's hand he was still aware of a kind of irritation with himself at being involved in other folk's lives. This was not what he wanted.

'Minty'll take care of your hoss, son,' Toween was saying. 'Come on in an' eat.'

41

Toween proceeded into the house and Dayton followed. The interior was a little better than the outside of the building. Someone, the girl called Minty, he guessed, had hung small drapes at the windows. The furniture was simple old-fashioned stuff freighted here years back, probably in a covered wagon. He wondered vaguely why Minty lived alone with her grandfather.

'Ain't a very big place,' Toween said, 'but Minty sure keeps it mighty clean.' He chuckled. 'A man can't even hawk an' spit on his own hearth nowadays. Times is changin', son. I come out here more'n ten year back. Nothin' here then but Injuns and buffler. Sure was a mighty nice place in them days.'

'*Those* days, grandpaw,' said the girl passing very hurriedly through the room in which they were now sitting. There was a log fire on the hearth and the two men sat one on each side. Toween in an old Ohio rocker, Dayton on a stool with a seat of tanned deerhide strips. The older man's eyes sparkled with sociability.

'''Tain't often we have a visitor hereabouts,' he said appreciatively and then reached down into a dark corner near his chair. His hand came up holding a stoppered earthenware jug. 'Reckon it calls fer a celebration, Mr Dayton,' he said and passed the jug across. 'It's corn liquor, son, an' mighty kind on the throat.'

'Thanks,' said Dayton and unstoppered the jug. It was strong genuine corn whisky. He drank and passed the jug back to Toween. The old man used it in the old backwoods style resting the base of the jug on his upper arm drinking with a quick wobbling of his pronounced Adam's apple.

'Grandpaw,' said a clear young voice from the doorway, 'you ain't supposed to be drinkin' thataway. The doc said you were to lay off hard liquor.'

The old man coughed and spluttered.

'Goddam it, girl,' he said, 'ain't I told you never to interrupt a man when he's drinkin'.' The girl retreated. Toween turned to Dayton, an apologetic look in his faded blue eyes. 'Not her fault. She's a good girl an' all she knows I've taught her, an' that ain't much, not by some folk's standards.'

'What happened to her ma and pa?'

'Both drowned in a flash flood in Nebraska, son. We came along the Oregon Trail from Independence. It was early spring an' a Chinook started to blow. Snow higher up melted too fast. We was caught in an arroyo, leastways her ma and pa were. Minty was along of me in the lead wagon an' we'd just cleared the lip of the gully when a great wall of water came rushin' down. They didn't have a chance. That was all of ten years back an' Minty an' I have been together ever since.'

'How do you get by?' asked Dayton.

'We run three-four hundred head of cattle,' said Toween. 'Ain't a very big spread as spreads go. The Tollers south and west of here run three thousand. Reckon we ain't been as lucky as we ought. We've had Injun trouble an' rustler trouble, too. I was throwed in the fall round-up and ain't been able to ride since. My leg was busted and wouldn't set right. Then we've lost two of our hands which leaves only me an' Minty an' a hombre called Cimarron who's more interested in the way his hair curls than in cattle. On top of that I'm in debt. The Tollers bought my note from the Bank. If I don't ante up within two weeks they'll seize my land. An' they can do it legal-like.'

'Why should they want your range? From what the girl said it isn't very big.'

'No,' said Toween. 'It ain't big but it's got the best watering for miles around an' the Tollers have had an eye on that for a long time.' He stared into the glowing heat of the fire and then continued.

'Y'see, son, I staked my claim here more'n ten years back. I saw the way things panned out then, with plenty of water coming down out of the Watenope mountains to the north an' I filed on that. Mark Toller didn't come in here until eight years after me. He had to take what was left, the range land west and south of me as far as Bridgerville. He cut me off from town but not from water and it's water he wants, my water.'

Dayton got up and walked restlessly across the room. It wasn't any concern of his. All he wanted was to ride on, right out of the territory, find a new place, a new job in which to forget.

He turned irritably towards the old rancher who anticipated him by saying, 'I was about to ask you if you'd consider workin' for us. But I ain't so old an' blind as not to be able to see you've got other plans, Mr Dayton.'

'I was figurin' on ridin' way over to Oregon,' said Dayton, and looking up he saw the door from the rear of the house open and a girl came in. At first he thought that he was about to meet a third member of the family and then, staring, he saw that it was the girl

Minty. She was carrying dishes which she set down on the home-made table. She looked different now. The levis and shirt had gone. In their place she was wearing a blue cotton dress and her tousled brown hair was now set off with a blue ribbon.

She stood there for a moment and then said, 'I couldn't help but hear what you said, Mr Dayton. Reckon Oregon must be kind of a nice place. You talked once of goin' over that way, Grandpaw.'

'Guess one place's as good as another,' the old man said. 'It ain't the place. It's the folks as counts.'

'Folk like the Tollers,' snapped the girl and went out. The old man blinked unhappily.

'In this world, son, there's sons of bitches, almighty sons of bitches and goddam ornery sons of bitches. The Tollers come high in the last class. Things hev been mighty hard for Minty since they came along,' he said. 'Guess they make her feel onsartin and that's a bad thing for a young gal like Minty. She's only eighteen come spring.'

She returned as the old man finished speaking, this time with platters of food, steak and potatoes.

'Come an' git it,' she said briskly. 'It won't be hot for long.' They sat up to the table and ate silently and hungrily. Dayton realised that he had eaten little or nothing for long hours and was grateful for the hot food.

When they had finished the meat and potatoes she went out for apple-pie and coffee. With his second cup Dayton rolled a cigarette. The old man watched him.

'You aimin' to go in for the cattle business, Mr Dayton,' he said at last.

'I'd like to,' said Dayton. 'I lived on a farm when I was a kid.' They had been lively carefree days till the war came and everything disappeared in the flame and roar of the guns.

'There's nothing to stop a man now,' said Toween. 'The Injuns is whipped or will be soon an' that'll leave the whole of this territory wide open fer ranchin'. It'll be a bigger thing than gold-minin'.'

'There was talk in Omaha about Crook going out against the Sioux,' said Dayton. 'It was said he'd have Custer an' the Seventh with him.'

'Custer's a big wind,' said the old man. 'They need someone a mite less vain an' a mite more clever than Yellow Hair to make medicine with a wily old buzzard like Sitting Bull or wild warriors like Crazy Horse an' Gall.'

Dayton threw the butt of his cigarette into the glowing embers of the fire.

He stood and stretched.

'Reckon I'll be pushing on,' he said.

Toween looked up at him.

'It's well on into dusk, son,' he said. 'You're welcome to bunk down here for the night.'

Dayton looked across at the girl. She nodded her head.

'It'll be warmer here than out in the hills,' she said. 'There's three empty bunks out in the bunkhouse.'

'You've got another man working for you?' queried Dayton.

'Yes, Cimarron,' said the girl. 'He won't interfere with your sleep none.'

She looked at her grandfather. 'Where is he, grandpaw?'

'Went out after some strays in the early afternoon. Ain't showed up since.'

'I'll take you up on your offer, Mr Toween,' said Dayton. The girl moved across to the wall and unhooked a kerosene storm lamp. Dayton struck a match and lit it. He took it from her, aware of her long solemn-eyed scrutiny as their fingers touched. He realised suddenly and with some surprise that she was a pretty girl.

He went to the door then and was about to draw the bolt when he turned and said, 'I thank you both kindly for your hospitality.' Grandfather and grandchild were standing with their backs to the fire, watching him go, almost with a kind of sadness in their eyes, almost as if deeply reluctant to see him leave. He picked up his saddle-bags and his Winchester.

'Ain't nuthin' at all,' said Toween quietly. 'Glad to have somethin' to offer even though it ain't much.'

'Goodnight,' said Dayton and went out into the darkness. He had spotted the bunk-house when they first rode in and now he made his way there, the lantern throwing its pale circle of light on the muddy ground. He found the door and pushed it open with his boot, cautiously. He had long since learned never to enter a strange room over-hurriedly. He held the lantern at arm's length and scanned the interior. The bunkhouse was empty save for its four bunks. Above the upper of the left-hand pair a shard of mirror was nailed to the log wall. A tin-type of a girl was tucked between the mirror and the wall. The bunk would be Cimarron's. He carried his gear across to the lower bunk on the right of the room. He unrolled his blankets and laid them out on the tick. Then he sat down, yawning. The story Toween had told was familiar enough. The small man clinging desperately to something of value that the big man wanted. It was as old and bitter as the history of man. Slowly he pulled out a sack of Bull Durham and began to roll a cigarette. It was none of his affair. All he had to do was to ride on next morning, get clear of other folk's troubles. He found a match in his vest pocket and snicked it alight on his thumbnail. He inhaled the smoke deeply. There was something mighty likeable about Toween. And the girl too. Strange life for a growing kid.

Thinking suddenly froze into a complete awareness of his surroundings. His big right hand crept to his gun-butt. The noise had come from close outside. Suddenly the door came open with a crash and a man came in. He was tall, well knit, except for his face. The features were loose, crafty, deeply marked with self-indulgence. His eyes shifted too much.

He said, 'Howdy! Toween said I'd find you in the bunkhouse.'

Dayton stood up.

'You're Cimarron, I reckon. I rode in with the girl. I'll be riding on tomorrow.'

'Ah! the girl. Little Miss Minty!' The newcomer grinned wolfishly as he shrugged out of his coat. 'As to ridin' on I reckon that's a good move on your part, mister. This goddam place's about to fall apart at the joints. I dunno why I stay.'

Dayton had his suspicions, but he kept them to himself.

'Reckon I'll turn in,' he said and sitting down began to pull off his boots.

Cimarron produced a pocket comb and began to pretty up his black curly hair. Dayton unbuckled his gun-belt and laid it close to hand on the inside of the lower bunk. Then he lay down on his blankets, flat on his back.

After a time Cimarron finished attending to himself and blew out the lantern. Dayton listened to his movements as he got into his blankets. Then there was silence.

He must have fallen asleep. The sudden gunshot close at hand brought him rigid and tense on his right elbow. There was a minute's absolute silence and, with feverish haste he buckled on his gun and thrust his feet into his boots. He heard the other man across the room breathing heavily.

Dayton whispered through space, 'I'm goin' out.'

He felt his way to the door and reached for his Winchester leaning against the wall. He put his hand up to the latch. There was a sudden flurry of gunshots then, light and heavy, revolver and rifle fire. A window on the far wall splinted into fragments. He waited.

'Who could it be?' he whispered over his shoulder.

'The Tollers,' came back Cimarron's reply.

Dayton crouched near the door, thinking fast and angrily. The raiders seemed to be concentrating on the ranch house. Twenty-thirty yards from where he was. He'd have to make a run for it and get there. There was more gun-fire, a drum-roll of shots. Slowly he raised the latch and opened the door gently. He peered out through the two inch space. Even as he did so light bloomed yellow-tawny from somewhere on the left. He widened the aperture. They had set fire to a small hay-stack and its ruddy flickering light illumined the whole face of the ranch house.

He knew that he'd got to get in there with the girl and her grandfather. Holding the rifle in his left hand he flung the door wide open and ran crouching and zigzagging towards the rear of the Toween house. Shots followed, whining off the ground. But he was there in the shadow of the small stout building. He ran quickly to the rear, turned a corner and cannoned into a rising figure. He swung the rifle at the man's legs. There was a grunt of pain and the man went down. Dayton drew his Colt and brought the butt down on the man's head.

Vaguely he made out the shadow of a door and on this he rapped urgently.

'It's me, Dayton,' he said, speaking as loudly as he dared. There was a faint noise from within. Someone drew back a bolt.

'If you're tryin' to pull a fast one then think twice,' said a young voice. 'My gun's loaded in both bar'ls.'

The door opened slowly and someone behind fell back sharply.

'It's me, Dayton,' he said. 'I kinda figured you could use a little help.'

She said, 'Come in.'

He could make her out faintly in the darkness of the room.

'Where's your grandpa?'

'In the front room. He'll keep them Tollers dancin'.'

'Yes,' said Dayton. 'Still there's quite a lot of 'em, judging by the number of shots they've popped off.'

After rebolting the door, she turned and made her way into the room in which only an hour or so ago they had sat and talked.

'Keep your heads down,' said Toween. 'Guess that'll be Mr Dayton with you, Minty. I sure reckoned we could count on him.'

There was another volley of gunshots and they heard the slugs thud into the log walls.

'How many d'you figure there are?' asked Dayton. He had made out Toween's shape crouching in the lee of the left hand window.

'Eight or nine,' said Toween.

'I met one on my way over from the bunkhouse. He won't trouble anyone for a few hours.' He knelt down close to the bent figure of the old man. 'What're you aimin' to do?'

'Sit it out,' said Toween. 'Done it before. With Injuns.' He raised himself slightly, swung his rifle up and fired through the broken window. The shot drew the raider's fire. Dayton made his way across to the other window and laid his rifle across the sill. The haystack fire was still burning brightly and in its radiance he saw a running shape making for the corner of the ranch house. There was time enough and he made sure, with a slow even pressure of his trigger finger. The Winchester roared and the running figure threw up its arms and fell heavily to the ground.

'Good shootin', son,' sang out Toween and began to pump shots into the darkness where the raiders were hidden. In his haste and excitement he got to his feet. There was an answering volley of shots and suddenly Toween gave out a high gasping cry. He reeled back, dropping his rifle and fell heavily to the floor. The girl screamed and Dayton ran across to the fallen man. He knelt by Toween and supported him in his arms. Blood was oozing out of a hole in his shirt front spreading, soaking through the flannel. Toween's eyes opened, mild and blue. He spoke with great difficulty, his voice wheezing in his throat.

'Reckon it had to come. Had to come someday.' His head moved restlessly. 'Where's Minty?'

'I'm here, grandpaw. Right here. By your side.' The young voice was choked with grief and a terrible urgency.

'You'll be alone now, Minty.' His eyes moved away from her, focussed with difficulty on the face of Dayton. His words came with diminishing strength. 'Don't leave her

alone, son. She's mighty young. Don't...'
And then the words trailed off into a thin
incoherence and finally into nothing.
Toween's head rolled a little and Dayton
knew then that he was dead.

The girl seemed to sense it too and
suddenly she was on her feet and running to
the door. Before Dayton could stop her she
flung it open and screamed out into the
night.

'You've killed him! You've killed my
grandpaw. You murderers.'

The gunfire had stopped. Dayton came to
the door and grabbed the girl's waist. 'Come
in,' he said urgently. 'Come in.'

And then a big hard voice shouted at them
from the shelter of the trees.

'He got what was comin' to him. You'll git
the same if you don't quit by sundown.'
There was a moment's pause and then the
voice continued. 'If that's Dayton with you
then tell him he's bought into the wrong
game. Tell him to git out fast.'

Dayton registered with a slight surprise
their knowledge that he was there. The voice
was Brad Toller's. Standing there he heard
the movement of horses and knew they were
riding out. For a time he was aware only of
that and of the drum of hoof beats as they

rode away into the night. And then he heard the muffled weeping of the girl. She had moved back and was leaning against the door post, her head resting on her forearm.

Cimarron came out from the bunkhouse as they stood there.

Dayton took her gently by the hand and led her back into the ranch house. He lit a lamp and carried the dead Toween into the inner room. Then he returned to wait with her through the long night for the bitter light of dawn.

CHAPTER FOUR

Dayton walked out of the room in which Toween had died just as dawn pushed pale fingers of light above the eastern ranges. The girl exhausted with grief had fallen asleep with her head on the table. He had sat watching her for a long time reliving his past, building the future irrevocably out of the present.

He stood now in the first grey light watching dark shapes slowly becoming recognizable. His vague plans were in ashes now. Something would have to be done for Minty Toween, alone and at the mercy of the Tollers. It was never life alone that was such a hard and bitter affair but the knowledge of life and death, the inseparables. He had known that in the burning twisted horror of Appomattox and Vicksburg, in the many deaths on many trails since then. But for her this was the first knowledge.

He turned back into the room, crossed it light-footed and went on into the ranch kitchen. He found a pot of cold coffee and some tin mugs. He started a fire and heated the coffee. He found biscuit and cold bacon. While the coffee was heating he found sugar and milk. Then he loaded the lot onto a tin tray, added the hot coffee and went back into the parlour. He put the tray on the table and the girl stirred a little. He put his hand on her shoulder and wakened her gently.

Her head came up and she opened her eyes. For a long moment she was wholly still and then her eyes clouded as the memories of the night came back to her.

He said softly, 'Have some coffee, Miss Toween.'

'No,' she replied. 'I don't want anything. Nothing. Nothing at all.'

But she watched him pour coffee into both mugs. He added sugar and milk to hers and left his black. Then he waited patiently, rolling himself a cigarette, until at last she reached out a hand and began to drink. The hot coffee brought colour to her cheeks and her eyes lost something of their apathy.

He said at last, 'What would you wish me to do about your grandfather? We can take him into Bridgerville an' wait on Sam Merlees' pleasure. Or he can rest here. It's up to you.'

She said very quietly, 'He loved his land

and would like to stay here, I reckon. We'll not make it a matter for the law. I'll give the Tollers back what they gave us in my own time.' She paused and sighed. 'Will you put him somewhere behind the house. I will come when you are ready.'

He went out at once and found spades in the toolhouse. The man called Cimarron came out of the bunkhouse and stood watching him as he selected a strong one.

At last he stepped forward and selected a spade for himself.

'Reckon you could do with a helpin' hand,' he said grudgingly. Dayton led the way to a spot behind the house and in the shade of a group of cottonwoods they worked silently for an hour digging a grave.

When it was deep enough Dayton returned to the house. He found a stout tarpaulin and in this he wrapped the body of the old rancher. Then with Cimarron's help he carried him out and laid him in the grave.

Minty came out when he called her and stood by the graveside.

'Will you say a prayer, please,' she whispered.

Dayton tried hard to remember the burial service as he had heard it in Omaha but the words came back to him only in disjointed fragments.

He said humbly, 'I can only remember the Lord's Prayer.'

She said, 'That will be enough. Grandpaw was never very set on church-going.'

Dayton said the Lord's Prayer and her voice uttered the old simple words with him.

They stood up.

Minty gave the two men her curiously direct look.

'Grandpaw Toween was a good man,' she said. 'He wasn't given to preachin' at folks an' he wouldn't want anyone to be preachin' about him. He knew about cattle an' makin' preserve an' if he did have rather a hankerin' after corn liquor, I figure the Almighty ain't goin' to be worrit about it.'

She stared down into the grave then with the tears running freely and with no more to say and the two men slowly filled the earth into the last resting-place of John Toween.

The girl preceded them to the house but she was waiting when they came in, waiting, now that it was over, Dayton realised, with a full warmer understanding that grief must end and life go on.

'This ranch is mine now,' she said firmly,

as they stood there.

'Won't be for long if the Tollers hev their way,' commented Cimarron.

'They'll have to kill me too to get it,' she said fiercely.

'They'll do that too,' said Cimarron. 'Why don't you cut your losses? Go back East. This isn't no place for a kid like you.'

And Dayton looking at her small grief-stained face, homely and gentle, was inclined to agree with Cimarron. But she turned her eyes on him then and in them was such a loneliness, such an unspoken demand for help that he could say nothing. It was then that they heard the hoof-beats of a horse. They turned, moving to the door and saw the solitary rider coming. There was something, even at a half-mile's distance, that looked familiar to Dayton. Then as the distance shortened he knew that it was Ep Rollins and as on many other occasions was puzzled by the man's uncanny gift for tracking him down.

He was close at last and they all watched him climb out of the saddle, lanky, thin almost to gauntness, his black hair long and loose almost to his shoulders. He tied his horse to a corral bar and came forward with outstretched hand.

'Howdy there, Will. Sure had a hard time tracking you from Bridgerville.'

'Howdy, Ep,' said Dayton. He half-turned to the girl. 'This is Miss Toween who owns this spread.' He waved a big hand towards the newcomer, 'My friend Ep Rollins.'

'Honoured to meet you, ma'am,' said Rollins gravely. 'Heard of you an' your Grandpaw. Never met him.'

'You ain't likely to, mister,' she said. 'He's dead.'

'This place was raided last night by the Tollers,' said Dayton hurriedly. 'They killed Toween.'

'So,' said Rollins quietly.

'If I could git the cattle to market,' said the girl, 'the price they'd fetch would more than pay off grandpaw's debts. His note don't fall due for over a week.'

'Where would you sell 'em, Miss Toween?'

'There's only Bridgerville,' she replied. 'An' to git there would mean crossing the Tollers' range.'

Dayton's mind worked fast. There was an alternative, another route, another market.

'No,' he said. 'There's not only Bridgerville. There's Warbonnet too.'

'Warbonnet!' exclaimed the girl. 'That ain't possible.'

'It's a hundred miles from here, Will,' said Rollins. 'An' a lot of it through Injun country.'

'I hadn't forgotten,' said Dayton. 'Nor the twenty miles of desert. I put it as the only way in which you can best the Tollers. I'm ready to try it if you're game to take the risk, Miss Toween.'

When the words were spoken he couldn't think why he had said them.

'I'll take any risk you like to ask, Mr Dayton,' she said.

He looked at her searchingly for a few moments and saw nothing but courage and reborn hope in her eyes.

'Let's work it out on paper,' he said. 'It's the only way I can get things clear.'

He turned indoors and on a sheet of wrapping paper with a stub of pencil he sketched out the route they would have to follow. The long dry trail, south-east across the desert. A swing east to cross the Montana Trail through forty miles of territory that, since 1868, had reverted to the Sioux and the Northern Cheyenne and then on through the hills to Warbonnet with its corrals and stockyards and cattle-buyers, its hotels and saloons.

'I know a man in Warbonnet,' said Dayton.

'He'll buy your cattle gladly at 18-20 dollars a head. Maybe more.'

'Who's goin' to trail the cattle to War-bonnet?' Rollins sounded dubious. 'You'll need six-seven hands for a chore like that.'

'I was countin' on you, Ep,' said Dayton.

'I ain't popular in Warbonnet,' said Rollins. 'Got into a mite of trouble there about nine months back. Could be if I poked my nose in there again they'd take the skin off it.'

'That's a risk most folks have to take,' said Dayton drily. 'What about you, mister,' he continued, turning to Cimarron.

The one Toween hand looked back uneasily, then spat. 'Reckon I'll buy in,' he said. 'There ain't much else to do.'

The man had a kind of courage or at any rate, recklessness, thought Dayton.

'I'm used to trailin' cows,' said Minty Toween. 'Been handlin' 'em since I was eleven years old.'

'It's no ride for a woman,' said Dayton shortly. Now that he'd taken on this foolhardy responsibility he wanted no additional burdens.

'I ain't a woman, mister,' came the tart response. 'And if you'll forgive my sayin' so, these are my cows an' if they're to be sold I'd kinda like to be in on the sale.'

'Reckon so,' said Dayton slowly. 'Only don't complain, Miss Toween, if the going gets rough.'

'I ain't the complainin' kind. I'd sure like to go. You don't have to treat me any different from a man.'

She wasn't much like a man, he thought, but they were her cows and anyway she had a whole lot of courage and resolution in her.

'Who's going to be boss of this outfit?' he put the question directly to her.

'Shucks, mister. It's as plain as the mountains up yonder. You naturally, who else?'

'You'll find me a hard-driving man, Miss Toween,' he said dubiously.

'That's what we want if we're goin' to git to Warbonnet.'

He looked away from her then and his questioning eyes sought those of Rollins.

'You in on this, Ep?'

Rollins gave him his long dark look. There was uncertainty in it and, Dayton thought, a shadow of something intangible, fear perhaps.

'I'll side you,' he said at last. 'I jist don't want to get mixed up in anything in Warbonnet. An', anyways, Will, as you know, I'm a lone wolf. But I'll ride with you and help poke the cow-critters along.'

Three men and a girl to drive three hundred cattle a hundred miles. It was a tall order but taller ones had been carried out before now.

'All right,' he said and then looked at Minty Toween. 'Where are the cattle?'

'If they ain't been too scared by all the gunplay,' she said, 'they're all within a few miles of here. They've been winter-grazin'. We would have driven up into summer pasture if all this trouble hadn't started.'

'We'll have to work fast if we're going to beat the Tollers. Your grandpa was due to pay up in about a week, you said.'

'That's right,' said the girl. 'Just ten days from now.'

'We'll start the gather now,' said Dayton. 'Ep and Cimarron and me. I count on you to provide grub and water, Miss Toween, enough for five days' riding. Each rider to carry his own. No chuck-wagon. No remuda. The horses'll have to last out the hundred miles.'

'I'll have it ready in two hours,' she said.

'It'll likely take longer than that to round-up three hundred head of cows.'

'They're mainly north-west of here,' she said. 'You'll find 'em bunched up in the draws and near the Teton Spring.'

And so without more ado they rode out to round up the Toween herd. They found most of them as she had said within a few miles of the home ranch. Each of them made his gather – anything from four-five cows to fifteen. They rode in chousing the cattle to the bed-ground they had selected, a flat jut west of the ranch house. By one o'clock they had all gathered in over two hundred head but Dayton was still not satisfied.

'These critters'll fetch twenty dollars a head in Warbonnet,' he yelled at the girl through the haze of dust that their riding had raised around the whole area.

She stamped her foot. 'Grandpaw's debt is under four thousand,' she yelled back. 'Two hundred will do.'

But he was obstinate and rode out again into the spring sunshine, Rollins and Cimarron with him. This time they were away for over two hours but they came back with seventy more that they'd found grazing in a small box canyon over ten miles east of the creek.

It was well on into afternoon now. Cloud had built up in threatening black masses overhead and just as they got in with the last bunch of cattle rain fell heavily. But they got the whole small herd together and Rollins offered to keep an eye on them while the others made their final preparations for the trail to Warbonnet.

Minty Toween had baked biscuit and made roast meat sandwiches in large quantities.

'There's canned tomatoes an' beans. There's bacon – not much an' a small sack of applies,' she said when they came into the kitchen. From a great pan on the stove she ladled out plates of stew and they settled down to meal that would ready them for the long trail ahead. When Dayton had satisfied his appetite, he went out, slicker-clad, to relieve Rollins who came in ten minutes later to wolf down the remains of the stew, potatoes and apple-pie.

It was well past four o'clock when they were ready to go. Minty looked dubiously out at the now sodden ranch yard. Rollins had gone off with the horses. It was a mad crazy thing they were going to do and she was responsible. She was the spark that had fired the three men with the wild impractical notion of a hundred mile drive through desert and Injun country and the Lord knew how it would all end. Her thoughts turned easily to Dayton, the big hard man who'd saved her life in Bridgerville and who treated

her with such a cold politeness. She sighed
and then was afraid, suddenly. She half-
turned and saw Cimarron with Grandpaw's
corn liquor jug held high to his wide mouth.
His Adam's apple was wobbling hard and
whisky trickled from the corners of his lips
down on his shirt.

He saw her staring and lowered the jug.

'Just the stuff to start a fiesta with,' he said
and, grinning, advanced upon her. He
caught her before she could reach the door,
grabbed her in his long arms, wound them
about her and bent her in an arc under his
looming bulk. She cried out and beat her
fists against his chest. But his loose wet
mouth pressed down on hers, crushing out
the scream that rose within her. Then his
mouth moved down to her throat and his
big hot hands pried and preyed on her like
animals. She screamed once more and
heard the door crash open behind her.

She fell to the floor then as Cimarron
turned to face what was coming. It was Dayton again, his face black with rage. He
grabbed Cimarron's shirt with his left hand
and drove his right fist into the ugly snarling
face. Cimarron went over like a felled tree.
He was on his feet again in seconds, circling,
his eyes wildly searching for some weapon.

Dayton drove in again using both fists, a left to the stomach that curled Cimarron over frontwards and a hard uppercut with the right that uncurled him and laid him flat and groaning on the hard-packed earth floor.

'Get up,' said Dayton, but Cimarron's only answer was to roll moaning and crying onto his face.

'Please,' said the girl. 'Please don't hit him again. He'd been drinkin'.'

'All right. All right,' said Dayton breathing heavily. He looked down at the still moaning figure on the floor. 'Don't ever come near the girl again. Don't even look at her. If you do, by God, I'll kill you. Git.'

Cimarron weaved to his feet and went out. Dayton turned away then and looked at the girl, his face still white with anger.

'A woman only gets what's coming to her,' he said angrily. 'If you didn't flaunt your hips in those pants, maybe men would keep their hands off you.'

It was her turn now to go white and then scarlet with embarrassment.

'I ... I can't sit a hoss in a dress,' she said softly. 'An' grandpaw ain't been able to afford another pair of pants for me. He bought me these two years ago.'

She looked so utterly miserable that

something of his anger left him and to hide a reluctant smile he turned away from her, saying: 'Time to get that herd on the trail, if we're going to get to Warbonnet in five days.'

He went out then and did not see the tears that welled into her eyes nor the tremendous effort of will that stopped the flow and left her clear-eyed and maybe more than a minute older.

At Dayton's suggestion they bunched the herd and picked out a likely-looking steer as leader.

'With only four riders it gives us one at point, that's you, Miss Toween. Two for the flanks – Ep and Cimarron. I'll ride drag – an' eat your dust.' He paused. 'We'll push 'em hard for a few hours and camp late. We'll have to cover more than twenty miles a day.'

He stood up in his stirrups then and took one long look around. It was a pretty tough venture they'd taken on, with big risks for all and not much to be got out of it. He looked over at the man called Cimarron. A tough one with plenty of badness in him but he had horse-savvy as he had shown through the afternoon. Anyway it was too late now to fret over what folks were or weren't. There was nothing to be seen on the rain-swept land except the small brown herd, steaming faintly, heads down, and the three slicker-clad riders.

'All right,' he shouted. 'Get 'em under way.'

They got the herd moving, reluctantly at first, and then with a steady plodding progress. The cattle stretched out in a thin brown line, the lead steer well out in front. Rain was still falling but they moved on out into the twilight of the great plains.

Brad Toller had ridden back to the home-ranch in an evil mood. Dayton's fists had hurt but the hurt to his pride was harder to bear. His father was waiting for him, sitting in his rocker in the big living-room, exactly as he had sat now for long months since blindness had stricken him.

'You've been in trouble again, son,' he said.

'Yes,' said Brad Toller. 'But there'll be worse trouble for some folks I know.'

'Don't riddle me, son. What's been goin' on?'

Brad Toller gave him his version of the afternoon's events. The older man brooded on his words.

'The Toween place will fall into our hands like an apple in October. Ain't no call to go riotin' around. Toween can't pay his debt.'

'I aim to throw a scare into 'em,' said Brad Toller. 'And into Will Dayton, too, if he's still hangin' around that Toween girl.'

'Don't tangle with Will Dayton, son. He's the fightingest man west of the Missouri.'

'We'll see. We'll see,' said Brad Toller.

Brad Toller led his men over to the Toween place shortly after dark. He had no plan other than to speed the Toweens' departure. The girls cry of bitter grief giving the news that John Toween was dead sobered him down temporarily but by the following morning he had fully decided to keep his word. He'd have them out of there by sundown.

It was well after sundown when the Toller crew reached the Toween ranch for the second time in twenty-four hours. Coming across the hills and on to Toween range they had soon noted that there were no cattle grazing.

'Probably taken 'em up into the hills. That's not goin' to help 'em,' Toller said. They rode in cautiously through the thin rain. The whole place was curiously quiet. After much careful reconnoitring they approached the house and burst in only to

74

find the place deserted.

'They've cleared out,' said Toller triumphantly.

'They've taken the cattle with them,' said Jed Moss, coming in to the room.

'How d'you know?'

'I've moseyed around while you was bustin' in. The critters were rounded up a short way from the house and then driven off east.'

'East?' said Toller.

'Yup! East. I figure they've decided to drive 'em to Warbonnet an' sell 'em.'

Brad Toller stared at the T-Bar ramrod and read only a quiet conviction in the man's cold grey eyes.

'You're probably right,' he said grudgingly. And his mind immediately centred itself on an answer to this new and unexpected move.

'We could catch up with 'em in a coupla hours' ridin',' suggested Cal Bender, one of the Toller crew.

'No,' said Brad Toller. 'I reckon there's a better way than that.' He looked around the little circle of dark faces gathered in the Toween living-room.

'It'll take 'em four-five days to make the drive to Warbonnet. We'll catch 'em there or on the way out.' He looked at them again speculatively. 'I want two of you to watch

Dayton an' the girl in Warbonnet. You can hire a gun in town to get rid of Dayton and then you can grab the girl and bring her over here. I'll wait up at the line cabin. I know of a way of making sure that we don't go without water any more.' He looked at Jed Moss. 'You'll do, Jed, and take Cal Bender with you. Take your mounts by train from Bridgerville to Warbonnet an' bring her back, alive. You know what to do with Dayton.'

'Dutch Ivens is in Warbonnet,' said Moss.

'He'll do,' said Toller. 'You can draw the cash when we git back to the ranch and be on your way. Six days from now I'll be waitin' at the line camp on the upper pasture.'

CHAPTER FIVE

They made five miles due south-east before Dayton halted the herd. Occupied with the stragglers in the drag he had seen little of Rollins or Cimarron, other than a glimpse of an occasional shining rider skittering through rain and mud, swinging a rope at some balky steer with the wanderlust in its veins. He had seen nothing at all of the girl up at point but did not worry. They were still on her own range and she would be familiar with the terrain. The trail had lain across open country, well-grassed, old buffalo ground, to judge by the occasional wallow and piles of bleached bones.

It was well into night before she came galloping back from up front.

'We've got to the limit of our range,' she said to Dayton. 'The brush ends about a half-mile on an' runs down into the desert. From here on your guess is as good as mine.'

He said, 'All right. We'll camp here for the night an' try to cross the desert in one piece tomorrow.'

They heard a horse travelling then and Rollins joined them.

'Get Cimarron and bed 'em down for the night, Ep,' said Dayton.

'We'll ride up the other side,' he said to the girl.

It didn't take long. The cattle seemed only too ready to lie on the sweet grass. The rain had stopped at last and the stars were shining clear.

Later around a camp-fire they ate sparingly of the food they had brought. They drank coffee and lay back against their saddles. Cimarron was night-hawking the herd. They could hear him occasionally singing with an unexpected sweetness of tone a ballad of the cattle trails.

'I don't quite figure that hand of yours,' Dayton said to the girl. 'I mean Cimarron.'

'He's just a man,' she replied simply. 'He ain't a bad one. It's just that he tries to get what he wants, I guess.'

'One gets to wondering at times like this,' said Rollins, 'what it is that men do want. There's some want gold or land. Others want wine, women an' song.' He looked across at the girl. 'What do you want, Miss Toween?'

She did not answer at once. Instead with downcast eyes she pushed at the glowing embers of the fire with a mesquite branch. Then, suddenly, she looked up at Rollins.

'I'd like a good husband,' she said. 'A home an' children. I'd like to live in a place with other folks an' go to town once a week to market.' Her eyes slid away from him and he saw the long regard she gave to Dayton.

'I figure that's the best kind of wish, ma'am,' said Rollins. He looked at Dayton, his eyes sparkling now with an impish curiosity. 'An' what about you, Will?'

'I've got no wants, Ep,' Dayton said, with an edge of harshness in his voice. 'I've found that a man's wants when he gets 'em don't amount to much.'

Ep saw the girl's face flower young and alive in the warm fire-light.

'But you can't live all to yourself,' she said. 'That's a selfish way of living. Mighty lonely too, I reckon.'

'It's the best way,' he replied. 'Like that you get no set-backs, no disappointments. We live in a jungle world, and you survive only if you're hard.'

She said sadly, 'I don't believe it.'

He said, 'You will when you're ten years older.'

For a moment she looked as if she were

about to reply but she seemed to reconsider it and was silent.

'Reckon we'd better roll in,' said Dayton, some few minutes later. 'We've got to be on the trail at dawn. Cimarron will wake you in four hours, Ep and I'll take the last trick.'

Pondering on this he had his moment of doubt about Cimarron and the girl, but he dismissed it as unlikely now and rolling himself in his blanket he fell asleep at once.

When he awoke it was to find Ep Rollins bending over him, shaking him by the shoulder. He came out of his blanket chilled and stiff and went off, without speaking, to his horse. He saddled up and rode out to the herd. They were quiet. Nothing more than an occasional grunt from an old bull. He rode round to the far side. All was quiet. Nothing moved. Above, the stars shone clear in a cloudless night-sky. Somewhere out on the desert a coyote howled alone.

He rode on round the circle. It was strange, he thought. A man never knew how the cards would fall. If he had been asked on the train from Omaha what he would be doing in the next twenty-four hours the last thing he would have thought of would have been ramrodding a trail herd. And yet it was nothing new. A going back to what he had known before when he had come up the Texas trail to Wyoming, with the guns of the war still booming and roaring fresh in his memory.

He halted the bay on a small rise, crooked his right leg round the saddle-horn and methodically built himself a cigarette. When it was rolled he stuck it in his mouth and carefully sheltered the match flame in his hands to avoid scaring the cattle.

The fighting never died. A man fought the land or a balky horse, Indians or the labourers in the railroad gangs. And then his thoughts came back to Amy and to the failure of those bitter months in Bridgerville and how she had stood behind the lace curtains of their hotel room starting out with hopeless wretchedness at the bawling, brawling life of the town. Dead. The word pealed through his mind like a bell. Dead. And he had to go on alone. Slowly he crushed out the remains of his cigarette against his boot and whispering to the bay he moved on again around the circle of the herd. Slowly the last hours of night passed until at last dawn came grey and unobtrusive and he was able to go back to the sleeping forms of his three strange partners. He got a fire going, put on the coffee pot and then woke them to a new day.

They ate hurriedly and sparingly. No one had much to say at that early hour. They saddled up and got the herd moving off the brush land and down onto the desert.

'Keep 'em pointed due south,' he told Minty. 'We'll make 'em move as fast as we can.'

She rode off to point, letting her pony out to a gallop, dwindling to a small figure a half-mile from where Dayton rode. The herd thinned out into a long line and for a time, as they came tumbling down the grade onto the great stretch of sand, Rollins and Cimarron were kept busy with adventurous steers trying to slope off east or west of the trail.

There was little to attract them in the way of graze here. The grass had stopped where the brush ended and now there was only sand and spiny green-grey sage brush with occasional clumps of greasewood and mesquite bushes. As the sun rose they had the impression of passing rapidly out of a cold wet spring into the full heat of summer. The plodding cattle stirred up the dust and soon Dayton was forced to raise his neck-piece over his nose and mouth.

They plodded on, at well over two miles

an hour, in Dayton's estimate, until noon. Then he called a halt.

'You look like the masked rider of the plains,' Minty said as she rode in from point and saw Dayton with his neckpiece still in position over his mouth.

'You've been readin' Ned Buntline, ma'am,' said Rollins, grinning.

'It was one of Granpaw's books,' she said. 'He liked to read stories about the West. Said they gave him a good laugh.'

They made their meagre meal in the shade of some mesquite bushes, eating from a can of tomatoes, to slake their thirst. She sat down cross-legged to share the canned tomatoes and biscuit, aware of Cimarron's sullen gaze, of Rollins' quick laughter, of Dayton's quietness. He seemed to think of nothing but the chore in hand.

'Reckon if we get going again now,' he said, 'we can make the other edge of the desert before nightfall.'

She laughed suddenly at his response to her thoughts and he gave her a swift dubious glance and then strode off to his horse. Minty feeling curiously damped, mounted her pony and rode off to her position.

'I'll ride drag,' Cimarron offered and Dayton, surprised, said, 'Thanks.' He swung the bay over to the right flank and the drive was on again.

A small wind blew up as the afternoon wore on, and conditions worsened considerably. Minute sand particles hissed and swirled around them, whipping painfully against the skin. It slowed up the cattle which tried to turn down wind and had to be repeatedly choused back into line. Heavy black thunderheads were gathering in the East and Dayton eyed them with suspicion. If they broke there was no telling what the herd would do.

They rode on and thunder rumbled heavily in the eastern hills. Large spots of rain splashed lazily into the trampled sand. Cloud wrack passed sombrely overhead now. The next moment thunder crashed like big guns firing. The lightning forked down towards the desert in a great crackling flash. Dayton watched the cattle. Their heads came up and they lowed with fear and doubt. They were within a hairsbreadth of trouble now. It came with the next resounding crash of thunder.

The cows began to bunch and then run, their hooves adding a drumroll of sound to the thunderstorm above them. And then Dayton remembered that the girl was riding point. Her pony was good and she could outride the cattle, he thought, but one false step into a prairie-dog hole and she would be lying right in the path of the herd.

He whipped his spurs into the bay's satiny sides and the animal leaped forward into a dead run. Dayton rode up the right flank of the running bawling herd, aware as he went that they were now in full stampede. Once across the humped and heaving backs he thought he had a glimpse of Ep Rollins riding level with him. The rain swept down in a lashing torrent and thunder beat out its tremendous rhythm in his ears. He waited then for the next big flash to spot the girl. It came and he saw her well up on the stampeding cattle. Two hundred yards maybe, he judged. He was now up with the leaders of the stampede and he rode in towards them, seeking to head them off but their fear of the thunder was greater than their fear of man and they roared on. He turned his strained eyes once more to the flying figure of the girl at point and even as he did so what he had feared happened in a flash. Her pony stumbled and threw her over its head.

Dayton yelled once, spurred savagely and the bay leaped forward. They headed straight for the small fallen figure, reaching her in seconds. She was already on her feet and all he could see as he came in to a quick sliding stop was a small white frightened face.

He yelled, 'Get up behind,' and held out a hand. She managed it, swinging into position in one leap. He gave the scared horse its head but the steers were already up on them. A huge old longhorn swung its head savagely towards them but the bay was gathering speed and they pulled away then out of the track of the stampede. When he was sure that they were safe Dayton pulled up. He half-turned in the saddle to see how she was faring. She grinned at him and suddenly looking at her urchin face he was overwhelmed with exultant laughter, laughter that stopped all speech until at last he let her down on to the sand and climbed out of the saddle.

'Reckon,' he said, still laughing, 'this business of savin' your life is becoming a habit.'

'It's mighty reassurin' to have a handy man around,' she said smiling at him.

It was a moment, the first, of pure good humour. And they stood for a little time smiling at each other as if both had suddenly come across something worth while.

Ep Rollins rode up then.

'Sure good to see you folks,' he shouted. 'I

thought for a twitch you was gone geese.'
The thunder had died down now to a
muted rumbling in the west and the lightning had lost its virulence. Cimarron joined
them and Minty remounted behind Dayton.

It was late afternoon now and they rode
on towards the now visible hills. They were
maybe an hour's ride from there, Dayton
thought.

He said, 'Keep your eyes skinned for the
pony.'

They found it a quarter of an hour later
grazing unconcernedly in a small draw.
Minty mounted and they rode on, all of
them staring out over the sunset-lit flats for
some sign of the stampeded cattle. They
came in sight of them at last, clustering
round a water-hole, drinking thirstily, tired
and their fears all run off.

'It's all upgrade from here on,' said
Rollins. 'That's helped slow them down.'

'We've reached the end of the desert,' said
Dayton. 'But there's still a long trail ahead.'

'A smoky one at that,' commented Rollins.
'Take a look over to the east.'

They saw then the unmistakable smoke-
signals rising from two widely separate hills.

'Can't read 'em,' said Rollins, 'but I
watched 'em for most of the way across the

mountains. They're buildin' up for somethin' big. I'd say keep out of their way if we kin.'

Dayton said, 'If we run into any it'll be Cheyenne and Arapaho going north to join Sitting Bull. The war pipe went out as soon as Custer showed the way into the Black Hills.' He looked at the girl and saw that she was troubled by their talk.

'It's not too late to turn back,' she said, staring at them, solemn eyed.

'If you're game to take a chance on the cattle an' maybe on your own life then I vote we drive on,' said Dayton.

'I'm game,' said Minty simply.

'Count me in,' said Rollins.

The eyes of all three of them turned on Cimarron.

He said sullenly, 'I've come this far. Might as well see the thing thru'.'

'We'll make camp here then,' Dayton said. 'The cattle won't give trouble tonight.'

They were close to the water-hole now and in the failing light they made a quick count. Three cows were missing.

'Could be they're on ahead some-place,' said Dayton. 'We may pick 'em up tomorrow.'

They made camp there on a rise near the water-hole. Cimarron built a small fire of mesquite twigs and greasewood. 'We can risk it,' said Dayton. 'The Injuns won't come over this way.'

Minty heated up bacon and beans and this with sandwiches and coffee restored them to a kind of warmth and the comradeship that flowers out of danger shared.

When Dayton had gone to take the first trick of night-hawking, Minty lay on her blanket watching the red embers of the fire. In two days he had lost something of the sombre bitterness that had seemed at first his only way of looking at things. She speculated idly on the cause of it, figuring that it might be a woman who was responsible. Women, she thought, were kittle-cattle, as Grandpaw used to say. The ones she had met on rare occasions in Bridgerville were either sour drudges, gossips or, like Lulubelle Anders, painted hussies who were worse for men than red-eye whisky. Suddenly she saw Dayton smiling down at a painted woman in his arms. A painted woman! Land Sakes! It wasn't a painted woman at all. It was herself and she could feel his strong arms holding her tightly. She remembered how strong they had seemed when he'd saved her with them in the stampede. An enormous sense of comfort stole over her and with them to shield her from the desert night Minty Toween fell asleep. On her face there was a smile of absolute content.

CHAPTER SIX

At first light next morning they crawled out of damp blankets and sat around with mugs of coffee and watched Will Dayton draw them a map with his big forefinger in the sand.

'I rode this way two years back, comin' from east to west. There's a trail through the hills but there's no way round. There's a long line of them just ahead of us and then beyond that there's another range. In between is the Montana trail where we can figure on running into Indians.' He paused as if waiting for questions but none came. He looked at their silent serious faces and then went on.

'There's a way through ten miles long just east of here. That'll bring us out into the Montana trail. We'll have to push 'em hard and get across it to the further range before dark. We'll hole up there for the night and then push on across the pass. That'll bring us down onto the plains again.'

'If we ever get that far,' commented

Cimarron sourly.

'We'll get there, mister,' Minty assured him.

Dayton said, 'I'll ride point today. We'll need to scout ahead an' well ahead. So if you don't see me, don't fret. I'll be just around the next bend in the trail. You take the drag, Ep.'

He got up then and poured the remains of the coffee on the small fire. They saddled up and once more got the cattle on the move. And each of them now rode warily, knowing that what they were doing could end in disaster, in smoke and torture and death, like so many other ventures on the wartime plains in the 'Seventies, the smoky 'Seventies as someone had aptly called them.

At first the going was easy, across sagebrush flats and then on in the early morning warmth over lush grass prairie. There was little dust. The cattle were behaving well. Ahead of them lay the hills, green and well-timbered, gashed here and there with grey gorges and steep-walled canyons. Far up to the north a smoke column sent its messages through space. But that apart, all was quiet.

Too quiet, thought Dayton. One would welcome an approach to another kind of territory, with stagecoaches running, farms and cattle grazing. He suddenly realised that they were doing a crazy thing. That was a young girl riding out on the left flank. His memory suddenly filled with vivid pictures of what he had seen along the trail, images of violence and horror, the tortures meted out by the Indians to their captives, the twisted limbs, the torn scorched flesh. On one thing he was resolved and that was to see that the girl should not fall alive into Indian hands.

He rode on in the soft spring morning dismissing the ugly thoughts. They were getting close to the hills now and not far ahead he could see the break where the long twisting valley began. It was through there that they must drive for all of the ten miles. He spurred the bay on and approached the way into the hills indirectly by climbing the hillside to the right of it. He was able then to command a view of the first mile or so of valley bottom. He reached the crown of the ridge and dismounted about ten yards short of it. Then he crept forward until at last he was able to peer over and survey what lay before them. He was almost surprised to discover nothing but the green empty space and the slowly mounting hillsides covered with scrub oak, alder and service berry, higher with pine and spruce. On the valley floor about half a mile away a small herd of pronghorn antelope were grazing quietly, their white rumps showing up clearly in the early sunlight. That, he thought, was a good sign. The pronghorn would not be grazing like that if there were Indians anywhere near.

He went back then and looked out across the flats to the approaching line of cattle, now about a mile away. He could just make out the figures of the three riders, swinging out occasionally from the herd and then back into position, the cattle plodding steadily through the sage-brush and over the grass vividly green in the late April sun.

They were closer now and he rode down from the ridge and joined the girl out on the left flank.

'They seem slow once you get out ahead of 'em,' he said as he joined her.

She gave him her usual quiet direct look.

'Ain't no good, grandpaw used to say, bein' fiddle-footed about cattle. You just have to think yourself inside 'em as though tomorrow ain't never goin' to come.'

He said, 'Maybe I'm too restless to be a good trail-driver. Comes of too much scouting around and ahead for the railroad,

I guess.'

'How long did you work for the railroad, mister?' asked Minty.

'Best part of eight years,' he said.

'Must hev been tough work,' she commented.

'It was. All kinds of men and women too.'

'Women!' Her eyes were suddenly curious.

'Not your kind of woman.' His eyes stared ahead into the vivid jumbled past. 'The women who follow the Hell on Wheels, dance hall girls, soiled doves, there are all kinds of names for 'em.'

'You sound as if you was angry at them.'

'I am,' he said. 'They don't deserve the name of woman. They're just painted jezebels, rotten right thru'.' He realised, even as he spoke, that he was saying things he had never said before, that he was going contrary to all his usually broad-minded ways. Maybe it was the memory of Amy and of her severe strictures that now spoke from within him.

He was aware that she was studying him closely and he sought to change the conversation.

'We're pretty near the valley trail here,' he said. 'I'll just mosey on ahead and see if all's quiet.'

He took the bay on up the line of cattle

95

then, got well ahead and found the open valley as he'd seen it before from the ridge, completely quiet.

He rode back and helped drive the cattle in and then once again went ahead to point. He went far ahead then on his second scouting trip covering about half of the valley's length, approaching bends in the trail with caution, watching the hillsides for the smallest sign of hostiles. There was nothing. No hint of danger.

He dismounted under a rocky outcrop in a narrowing of the valley. A vantage point that gave him a clear view of the trail behind and ahead. A small creek tumbled down out of the hills here, made a pool and slid off east towards the other end of the valley. He tethered the bay and rolled a cigarette. Then he leaned back against the warm rock face and let the accumulated tension of the last few hours flow out of him. It was good there, good as the life of earth and the quietness can always be. It suddenly seemed to him that the big questions that a man was always asking could be answered that simply. You made the most of the moment, of the feel of a horse moving surely under you, of the blue camp-fire smoke in the dusk, of the tall timber and the fine swift-flowing rivers. There wasn't much else. He finished his cigarette and ground out the butt with his boot-heel. As he did so the first of the cattle lumbered into sight well down valley and he waited while they covered the mile between them.

As they came closer he saw that they were beginning to lather in the heat of the day. He looked at his watch and found it was close to noon, and time to call a halt. So far, he thought, they had been lucky with nothing more than a stampede to reckon with. And even that had been in their favour. He wondered how long the run of luck would last, how long before it petered out.

The cattle scenting water rumbled up and crowded round the pool. Cimarron watered the horses. Minty Toween collected their canteens and filled them from the creek above the pool. They stood around eating dry sandwiches, drinking water. It was a welcome rest but Dayton broke it up within twenty minutes.

He simply said, 'Let's ride,' and went over to the bay. It was rested now and ready to go. He climbed into the saddle, calling out, 'Get 'em along as fast as they'll go,' and rode on up the valley. He decided to make for the exit to the Montana trail, riding again with wariness, on through the heat of the afternoon, his eyes questing the hill tops, his ears taking in every sound. There was still nothing to alarm him. The valley floor was harder, dustier here. And then after two hours some trigger-quick sense of danger halted him not over half a mile from the exit into the hard stretch of the Montana trail.

At first he could not figure out what had brought him to a stop. And then he knew that he had smelt dust in the air, dust disturbed not very long back. He looked around for a sign and, a few minutes later, found it. The tracks of an unshod Indian cayuse. Its rider had headed down out of the Northern hills and on up the valley to the east. A solitary rider, maybe a scout. Dayton rode cautiously on, following the tracks along the narrowing valley towards the rocks that piled up near the way out. He came in close to them at no more than a walking pace. And again some sixth sense came to him then. He half-turned and saw the naked figure plummeting down upon him from the twenty-foot high rock. His attempted swerve came too late. The impact was tremendous and he fell off the bay with a bone-cracking impact on the hard ground.

The two men rose almost face to face and

Dayton butted his head hard into the war-painted features of the big Cheyenne warrior. The man grunted with pain and swung a knife straight at Dayton's throat. Dayton side-stepped and drove a murderous right into the Indian's ribs. It knocked the man off-balance and taking advantage Dayton leapt on him, grabbing the Indian's knife-wrist in his own left and twisting it brutally. Suddenly there was a snap and the man gave a thin cry of pain. He fell heavily into the dust and Dayton following through seized the knife and plunged it deep into the fallen man's throat. Blood spurted out soaking into Dayton's shirt. He drew back then, tense, listening, breathing now with painful difficulty after the fall.

Nothing stirred in the rocks around him. Somewhere above in the softening golden light a bird sang clearly. He looked down at the body of the dead Cheyenne. It would have to be hidden and well-hidden too: or they'd have a hornet's nest of hostiles round their ears. There was also the problem of his pony which would be somewhere close at hand. He cast around for some hiding-place and then higher up on the hillside he thought he saw it in a large rock standing man's height over what looked like a shallow depression. It might be the answer.

Breathing with increasing pain he began to drag the Indian off the main trail up the slope of the hill towards the rock. The dead Cheyenne was heavy and Dayton soon felt the sweat gathering on his forehead and back. It took nearly ten minutes to reach the rock and hastily he began to scoop a shallow grave with his knife and hands. The rock looked as though it could be rolled over without much trouble. He laid the Indian in the hole at last and turned to the rock. At first it seemed to be too firmly embedded to move and then, straining his whole weight against it, he felt it give slightly. He eased off wiping the sweat from his forehead with the cuff of his shirt. Calculating the position carefully he heaved at it again and felt it move ponderously and then come down flat onto the dead body in the shallow grave.

He turned away then faintly sickened by what he had had to do. There was still the question of the dead man's horse. He angled across the hillside towards the point where the Indian had waited in ambush. And there near a clump of juniper stood the Indian's cayuse. It was either shoot it or hide it. The noise of a shot might give them all away if there were others in the neighbourhood. One couldn't just let it run. He moved slowly towards it and succeeded in grabbing its head rope. The easiest way out was to take it with them, keeping it captive till they were out of danger.

He returned to the valley bottom. It was strange, he thought. You had to kill a man to be sure. You could spare a horse. He tethered the pony to a tree just off the trail. Then he called the bay, climbed into the saddle and moved slowly towards the exit from the valley. At first he could only see the broad stretch of flat land before him and then as he emerged from the hills he took his cautious survey of the northern and southern stretches of the trail. At first he saw nothing and then moving out a little further he had to rein in sharply. Not more than a mile down the trail the conical tipis of an Indian camp stood up unmistakeably above the level ground. Ten-fifteen lodges, and that would make a sizeable band of Indians. And that put paid to any idea they might have of getting the cattle across the Montana trail to the second range of hills.

He reined the bay and headed back into the valley. The cattle were in sight as he rounded the first bend and he made for Minty Toween who was riding well forward on the right flank of the herd.

He said, 'There's Injuns camped out on the Montana trail. We'll sure have to think again. I ran into one of 'em at the bend in the trail ahead.'

He saw her eyes staring at the red splashes of blood on his shirt.

'What happened?'

'I had to kill him,' said Dayton.

She reined in and he watched the shadow of fear in her small kindly features.

'Help me halt 'em,' he said and they circled the tired herd to where Rollins waited on the other side. The cattle started grazing willingly enough and Dayton gave Rollins the news.

'Can't figure how we're goin' to get past an Injun camp,' he said.

The girl said, 'There's a way.'

Both men turned their full attention on her.

She said, 'Injuns don't like the night. They bed down an' wait for the dawn before they start raisin' hell, or huntin' or travellin'. I guess we could get the cattle across the valley in the dark.'

'It's an idea,' said Rollins. 'A mighty good idea.'

'We could try,' said Dayton. 'There's no

other way that I can see.'

They were joined now by Cimarron who listened as the plans were made.

There were two hours of daylight left and that with twilight too would have to be waited out. There was nothing they could do but sit and pray that no footloose Cheyenne would happen on their halting place and get away to rouse his fellows. They must watch the bend in the valley behind which the cattle were screened from anyone passing along the Montana trail. The two hours' rest would give the cows a breather. They'd be the readier to travel thru' the dark width of the main trail.

All four of them then prepared to sit out the long wait for darkness and all of them felt the steady building up of inner tension as the minutes crept slowly by. The setting sun lit up the valley floor for one brief golden moment and then disappeared behind the western hills. Ep Rollins sat on a rock whittling a stick and whistling tunelessly. Cimarron, hunkered down in the dust, smoked continuously.

Minty wandered across to where Dayton sat watching the darkening hills.

She said, 'I'm sure sorry I got you folks snarled up in all this trouble.'

Dayton kept his eyes on the hill slopes and replied, 'If it isn't one kind of trouble, Miss Minty, then I guess it's another. It's what the Good Book says.'

'Man is born to trouble,' she said in almost mechanical response but her mind was more fully occupied with the warm and pleasing realisation that this strange aloof man had used her Christian name for the first time, even though he had prefixed it with the formal Miss. She sat there feeling happier than she had for what seemed years. In the last light of day with the hills plum blue and looking huge against the pale sky this was for her the best that had been. In her rapt happiness she was unconscious of his eyes slowly turned towards her. He saw her for the first time, not entirely as she had first appeared, a slightly grubby, unschooled waif of the plains, but as a girl who had an appealing honesty, a reliability, a deep reserve of strength. A very different person from Amy. Young, much too young, for a man of his years to be becoming interested in.

She turned to him again, painfully aware of his strong brown features, the big column of his neck, of his hands powerful even when relaxed as they were, one on each knee.

She said, shyly, 'Where was you born, Mr Dayton?'

He showed no sign of the surprise her question aroused in him.

'I'm a Missouri man,' he said softly. 'My father ran off from Ma when I was knee high to a grasshopper. I helped Ma work her holding till I was twenty and then when the war got hotted up I went into the Confederate Army.' He paused as if meditating on the war years and then resumed without mentioning them. 'When it was over I went south into Texas an' punched cattle. I was in some of the early drives from the Nueces up to Abilene and Wichita. I took on as trail-boss to a herd of three thousand in 1869 and drove 'em to Ellsworth. The owner paid us off and I rode north for the first time instead of south. Two months later I was buffalo-hunting for the railroad and then after three years of railroad building, hunting and Indian-fighting they put me in charge of the commissary for the extension from Bridger-ville to the mines. And that's where you met me, Miss Minty, just after I discovered that the railroad was finished as far as I was concerned.'

'You've had a mighty busy life,' she commented. 'It must be good to see so much.'

There was a faraway dreamy look in her eyes. 'I can remember the long drive up the Oregon Trail an' I've been to Bridgerville a few times every year. I ain't seen much else.'

They sat in the silence and darkness gathered swiftly around them. She said suddenly, 'Reckon a girl like me must seem plumb ignorant to a man like you.'

'Knowledge ain't everything, Miss Minty,' he replied. 'Leastways the knowledge folks get in towns. I figure there's more to be said for horse-savvy than there is for book-learning. It never yet made people anything but money.'

'A woman,' she said, 'wants to know a whole heap more than how to cook flapjacks and how to wash denim overalls. There's a lot of things a woman misses just livin' on a ranch.'

'You stick to flapjacks and denims,' he said seriously. 'It's a better life than you'll ever have once you get fancy notions from livin' in a town.'

There was a silence then but it was a happy one for Minty Toween. She could have sat there talking with him till the cows came home. And then she was aware that he was standing up.

'It's nigh on dark enough to move,' he said

and moved over to where Ep Rollins was sitting.

'Reckon we might push 'em over now, Ep,' she heard him say. She got up and joined them.

He went over and called quietly to Cimarron. The Toween hand came over to them and Dayton said, 'The Injun camp's about a mile or so down trail. We'd better string out all on one side an' keep 'em moving steadily. If one of 'em breaks away to the south let it go. Our only hope is that if the Injuns hear anything they'll think it's evil spirits on the move, not cows.'

He looked at them in the faint light of the stars. 'If the Injuns tumble to what's goin on,' he said, 'and if they attack, ride with all you've got for the other side. It's up grade most of the way once you git over the trail until you hit Lost Man Pass. We'll rendez-vous there if anything goes wrong.'

Again he paused and then asked if they had any questions. But they were all con-scious of a pressing need to get moving.

'Reckon we might move out,' said Ep Rollins. 'I ain't never made a drive by star-light before an' I'm sure honin' to know jest what it's like.'

They went to their horses, mounted and

moved towards the now quiet sleepy cattle. It took a few minutes to persuade them to get under way but at last it was done and the small cavalcade and the trail herd moved quietly down valley towards the unknown hazards of the Montana Trail.

CHAPTER SEVEN

At first they had difficulty in persuading the cattle not to lie down. And then, after an hour's gentle pressure, as they began to quit the shelter of the valley the herd settled down to its accustomed walk. Not without alarming incidents as when a big steer let out a full-throated bellow. It would be heard, of that there was no doubt. What the Cheyennes would make of it was anybody's guess. They rode on silently, with not much more than a prayer as Minty thought between them and discovery. But a prayer was often a powerful thing, she reflected and accordingly said one on the back of her tired pony.

There was just enough starlight for them to be able to see the slow-moving mass of cattle, bulking larger now by night than they seemed by day. Dayton looked away down trail to where the Indian encampment should be but he could see nothing.

Slowly the cattle plodded on across the wide trail. At one point they crossed old wagon tracks – all that remained now to show that the emigrant trains had once passed this way to the promised land. Dayton smiled grimly. There was plenty of land in the West but what promise it held for the would-be settlers he had sometimes wondered. A promise of unceasing toil and mighty small gains, hard unremitting work, few of the little pleasures of life or none, blizzards, Indians, death by rope or gun or arrow or at best by rheumatism.

Far over in the east there was a slowly growing radiance and then watching he saw the big silvery tip of the moon push up over the hill-tops.

From somewhere south of them a dog barked and then others joined in. For a moment he thought they might have heard the plodding hooves of the cattle. And then he remembered the moon and the way it affected dogs. The barking died away and there was silence, broken only by the heavy breathing of the cows. They were stopping now and trying to graze or lie down and all four riders were hard put to it to keep them moving.

Slowly, it seemed to Minty, almost minute by minute they plodded on and it felt dangerous even to breathe loudly. Somewhere up ahead of her she could make out the dark shape of Will Dayton, ten, fifteen feet out from the slow-flowing herd, more sluggish than a stream in high summer. It would be good if they got through now and sold the cattle. She could pay off Grandpaw's debt and have enough over to start again. She was stricken suddenly with the oddness of this thought. There had always been Grandpaw and now ... now she was alone! Who'd ever heard of a female cattleman, a cattlewoman. She laughed aloud at the word and sensed rather than saw Dayton turn in his saddle and look at her.

Riding about fifty yards to the rear of Minty, Cimarron nursed his resentment, still burning in him, towards the big fellow who'd hit him so hard his body still ached. And all for that goddam girl, Minty. And just because he'd made a grab at her. But he'd bide his time and the big fellow would learn that Cimarron wasn't the kind of hombre that took things lying down. No, sir. He'd show him a trick or two he'd learnt in Arizona that would last the son-of-a-bitch his lifetime.

And Ep Rollins bringing up the drag was aware of the terrain changing as the strange night drive moved slowly eastwards. The flat land of the Montana trail was yielding now to dark outcrops of rock. Soon they would begin to climb up onto brush land and thence on towards the Pass, a long way ahead, but once reached and they would be safe from hostiles. He had ridden this country for a long time now, always a lone wolf with few friends and many enemies – the men who seemed to resent his freedom, who wanted him to behave like everyone else. Since the war he'd never slept in a bed, never worked with other men, had played out his solitary hand and would continue to do so to the end. In Warbonnet someone had called him a rustler and soon in the Long Branch others had crowded round with the hanging look writ large on their ugly faces. Fear had crowded him into near-panic and when he left the saloon there were two dead men on the floor and the crowd was backed up snarling against the bar. He'd got away fast and shaken off a posse with the ease of one to whom the hills were home. And now like some zany he was walking right back into the lion's mouth. To help a friend. He'd go, he thought, as far as the cattle bed-ground and then he'd hit the trail fast.

They went on up-grade for another two

hours. Their eyes accustomed now to moon-light vision made out the brushland ahead of them. And Dayton at last called a halt. He whistled softly to the dim figure of Cimarron ahead of him and then reined in. The cattle needed no checking. Wearily they stood in their tracks or sank to the ground in a muted chorus of snorting and rumbling.

Dayton rode back to where Minty sat her pony.

He said, 'I figure we can well last out the night here. It's nigh on midnight now. That'll give us five hours rest. Then we'll push on fast again to get shut of this part of the country.'

She wanted to do her share of night-guarding the herd and said so but Dayton rejected it and the three men shared the five hours that remained of the darkness.

At first light Dayton who had taken the last two hours shook them awake.

They ate quietly with daylight no more than a faint suggestion in the east. They had the cattle moving before full dawn and then they were at last able to see where they were. The terrain was extraordinary. They were moving now up-grade along a broad swathe of green meadowland that stretched for several miles towards a dark stand of timber.

It was a slow almost imperceptible climb but after an hour, even in the dawn freshness the cattle began to labour.

Dayton let them take their time. While they covered the last uphill two miles he spurred on ahead. The crest of the hill was timber-crowned and into this he rode searching a trail for the herd. He found one west of the pines, leading down sharply through high-piled rock into a steep-walled canyon. The way through looked clear enough and he rode back to tell the others.

It was as he back-tracked through the timber that he heard the flat spanging echoes of gunshots. He spurred through the last screen of pines and came out on to the long slope leading down. The cattle were milling confusedly about a mile down-grade. A dozen Indians were hightailing it in a big loose circle around the herd. He saw the flash of a gun from somewhere near the herd and then a second on its heels. He put spurs to the bay and thundered down the slope, unlimbering his Winchester as he rode. The Indians saw him coming and two of them angled off to meet him. Dayton reined in hard, steadied his mount and took slow careful aim at the nearest of them. He fired and the man fell backwards off his pony as if a giant fist had smitten him. He turned his attention to the second and realised that it was too late for a well-aimed shot. The Indian was almost on him, lance levelled out for the coup. Dayton grabbed the rifle by the barrel and when the Indian was only five feet from him slung it hard at the war-painted chest. This unusual move took the Indian by surprise. The heavy rifle caught in his right arm and before he could rid himself of it Dayton had drawn his Colt and shot him out of the saddle.

Turning towards the herd he heard more shots fired. He dismounted, grabbed the Winchester and leapt once more into the saddle. He put the bay into a dead run straight towards the herd. As he drew near he could see what they'd done. Rollins, Cimarron and the girl had, at the first sign of trouble, ridden to the front and forted up in a small hollow off the trail. The Indians saw him coming and manoeuvred to meet him. There was a quick flurry of shots from the hollow and two of the Indians ponies went down. This left a gap in the Indian line and through this Dayton thundered on the bay. They saw him coming and stood up showing as much relief, he thought, as if he was a whole troop of cavalry. Impatience made him yell at them, 'Keep down.' He dismounted behind their position and joined them. The cattle he noted were jammed together in a big mill.

'Get your horses,' he said urgently. 'We'll drive the herd straight at the Injuns.'

They were all four up and away in less than thirty seconds. They circled the big jam of cattle and rode in at their rear with guns blazing. Somewhere in front the mass broke and began to run and again within seconds they were stampeding wildly towards the Indians and the trees beyond. Dust boiled around them now and through it Dayton had one swift glimpse of an Indian on a rearing pony. He threw a shot at it and half saw it stagger and fall. Then he was past and straining his eyes for some glimpse of Minty Toween.

He spotted her then not more than a few yards ahead of him, lying along her pony's back. He rode closer to her.

'Scared?' he shouted.

'No,' she yelled. 'Take more than a few Injuns to make me scairt.' He grinned at her and they pounded on. The first of the cattle were among the trees now. He saw Rollins and shouted, 'Get in through the trees and down into the valley. I'll fight off any more that come this way.'

He reined in then and turned back. Dust was thinning out after the passing of the herd and dimly he could make out the prostrate bodies of what could be dead Indian ponies or cows or both. The attackers seemed to have given up. He scanned the broad spaces of the long green slope and could see no sign of them. Like all their kind they had the gift of disappearing into the land that was their own. He rode slowly down and counted four dead cows and three dead Indian ponies. Their owners dead or wounded had been carried off. He felt pretty sure of having killed two himself and the others could add at least one more. That should keep the hostiles away for a time. He had his long look at the scene of the fight and then turning his gaze towards the trees he saw another huddled shape on the ground that he had missed on his way down.

He cantered the bay over the hillside. It wouldn't be Minty or Rollins. He'd spoken to both not more than a few minutes back. It had to be Cimarron. Drawing near he saw that he was right. The Lazy T hand was lying face down on the grass. There was an arrow embedded deep in his back. Dayton dismounted. He knelt and turned the body gently and the sightless eyes of Cimarron stared blankly up into the blue morning sky. He leaned across and closed the lids. He heard a horse approaching. It was Rollins. When Rollins reined in, he said, 'We'll have to take him with us. We can't wait here.' Rollins said, 'His cayuse is up in the trees. We could tie him to it and bury him some place along the trail.'

'Get his horse, Ep,' said Dayton.

No one knew him, he thought. Nor where he came from or what name he was given. It wouldn't be Cimarron, anyway. He was just one of the many who drifted through the West, men without identity, forgotten within minutes of their violent deaths.

Ep returned with the dead man's horse and between them they fastened the body across the saddle of the scared and sweating mount. Then they rode on and joined Minty Toween who was waiting for them in the timber.

She watched them approach and knew the sadness of the moment. He had not been with them very long and his attempt to assault her was still fresh and painful in her memory but tears came into her eyes.

'We figured on moving out fast, Minty,' said Dayton. 'We'll bury him when we're out of Indian country.'

'Sure,' she said and turning her horse's head she rode with them on through the trees and down the steep trail into the canyon where her herd was now grazing peacefully.

They pushed on then through the long day stopping only for a standing meal and then moving on again slowly, painfully, through the warm early summer afternoon, until at last when colour began to change and flow in the hills they came out of the rough country and saw before them in the fading light the great flat stretch of the plains reaching out and out, it seemed to Minty, for ever.

While the cattle spread out into the high grass they found a point under the hill where they dug a grave for Cimarron. Dayton and Rollins wrapped him in his blanket and laid him in the shallow hole. Then they stood with Minty for a few seconds.

It was the girl who suddenly, impulsively, knelt down and spoke the words of the Lord's Prayer, the two men awkwardly kneeling beside her. When it was over they piled earth into the grave and then shifted rocks onto the low mound.

Dayton built a small fire and they boiled coffee and cooked the last of the bacon. Food was running low, he knew. They'd have to tighten their belts before the end of the trail was in sight unless next morning he could get a pronghorn in his sights.

They sat around the small fire, glad of its warmth as the chill of night came down on them, talking little.

And then Rollins staring into the small red glowing heart of the fire asked Minty what she aimed to do when the cattle were sold.

'Reckon I'll set up in business again,' she said seriously. The two men stared at her. She was fully aware of this gaze and glad that her blush was hidden in the dark cloak of night.

'The cattle business,' she said. 'What else do I know anything about?'

Neither man spoke for a moment. But she could see them mulling over her words in the heavy deliberate judging way men had.

'Kinda tough work for a woman alone,' said Rollins.

Dayton made no comment but she was aware of his gaze upon her. His silences she had observed were fuller of meaning than the words other men used.

'You don't figure there'd be much in it,' she said, aiming her words directly at him.

He drew meditatively on the cigarette he had rolled after eating and stared down at its red tip.

'No,' he said at last. 'I don't think you'd stand a chance, not with neighbours like the Tollers. They'd rob you blind, rustle you to a standstill within a month.'

'I'd fight them,' she said firmly. 'I'd hire men with guns.'

'You'd still not get anywheres,' he replied imperturbably. 'The Tollers have got more men, more money, more cattle, more range. You wouldn't have a hoot in hell's chance, Minty.'

'We'll see,' she said. 'We'll see.' But she said no more. Dayton yawned.

'We've got a long day ahead. Reckon we'd better sleep.' He looked at Rollins. 'Toss you for who's to take first trick with the cattle.'

They tossed and Dayton won.

'I'll take second turn,' he said.

'I could take a share of the nighthawkin',' Minty said.

'You'll need all the sleep you can get,' said Dayton shortly.

'Beauty sleep, Miss Minty,' said Rollins, winking at her.

She snorted with pretended rage but rolled herself in a blanket and with her head on her saddle was soon fast asleep.

CHAPTER EIGHT

Dawn was no more than a dim pallor in the east when Dayton rode back from the herd to wake Minty and Ep Rollins. They were low on food now, with only a few spoonfuls of coffee, two tins of tomatoes, a piece of rather tired bacon and some flour. He got a fire going and cooked sparingly. Then he went over to the blanket-rolled figures on the ground.

When they were awake and rubbing the sleep out of their eyes and the stiffness from their limbs he said,

'I figure we've got over twenty miles between us and Warbonnet. Maybe more. We're short on grub. The next twenty-four hours will be the worst.'

'Won't be the first time I've gone without grub for a day,' said Rollins. 'Life's always springing some little reminder on a man.'

'Reminder?' said Minty sleepily.

'Reminder not to get too plumb satisfied.'

They settled down to their frugal breakfast, making the most of the hot watery coffee. Away to the north the snow-covered peaks of the Wind River Mountains rose stark and grim in the early light.

'Grandpaw used to say that a man could live on water for a week without grub,' said Minty.

'There's always plenty of that in the Territory,' said Rollins.

They rolled their blankets and saddled up with dawn still spreading its rose-red flush across the sky. Then they rode out to the cattle and with much snorting and rope wielding got them on the trail once more.

Dayton rode out on the far left flank of the herd. Now that danger no longer threatened them he had time to think, time to let the memories come flooding in and even as they came engulfing him in the old sadness and depression he was aware that for nearly three days he had been free of them. But they were back again, the touch of a hand, the faint melody of a voice.

The cattle plodded on through the rising warmth of the morning, raising dust in a small steady cloud that clung behind them to the trail along which they had come.

About high noon they began to run and Dayton knew they'd reached Bear Creek. They slaked their thirst and prodded the cattle on, across the endless plains, with little more than the whitening bones of dead buffalo to break the monotony of the rolling green expanse.

Minty Toween came across to him once.

She shouted, 'How far you aimin' to get by sundown?'

'Maybe as far as our destination,' he called back. 'We're making good time.'

She rode away back to her position on the other flank, suddenly elated at the prospect. The venture had been a success after all. The Tollers had given up, hadn't even made a try.

There was a range of low hills ahead of them and they reached the ridge by mid-afternoon. The ridge ran north to south. They sat their horses looking out over the eastern plain. Sunlight spread out from behind a cloud and then she saw a faint smoke rising from the plains.

'Is that it?' she asked, pointing.

'That's Warbonnet,' said Dayton.

'How far?'

'Ten mile – maybe more.' He looked at her. 'We could make it by late evening.' He turned to Rollins. 'You game to press on, Ep?'

'Yup,' said Rollins.

'You, too, Minty?'

'Reckon so,' she said and clamped down on the sigh that rose behind her words. It puzzled her. Why this sudden regret that it was almost over. Covertly she looked at Dayton and knew where the reason lay.

'Let's move then,' said Dayton.

For a few moments before putting spurs once more to her tired mount she sat motionless allowing herself the small luxury of simply watching him. A tall hard-looking intractable man riding off towards the left flank of the cattle.

And once more the herd was pushed on at a slow three miles an hour towards the cattle town ahead of them. After four hours the lead steers emerged from a gully and the three riders could see ahead of them – no more now than three-four miles – the sunlit shapes of buildings. The cattle plodded on across the grassy slopes and then an hour later Minty could see more. High, false-fronted clapboard houses, barns, corrals – all clearly outlined in the last light of the sunset. Then the colour faded and the town began to change, became pale and ghostly and then seemed to blend and blur with the formless twilight of the surrounding prairie.

About a mile from town they reached

what Dayton considered a suitable bed-ground for the night. He halted them there on an indeterminate flat on the western outskirts of Warbonnet, near a swift-running creek.

Rollins elected to stay with the cattle and they left him all that remained of the provisions – enough, he said, to last him till next morning when Dayton promised to be back with the cattle-buyer he knew.

'We'll be at the Drovers, Ep,' he said, as they sat their ponies there in the thickening twilight.

She said, 'I reckon I could use a bed after the last three nights.' It was the kind of direct understatement that he was getting used to from her. Momentarily he looked at her, half-wondering at the strength and endurance she carried in her small compact frame. Then he swung their horses' heads in the direction of the town and away from the bunched-up weary cattle. A hundred yards from the bed-ground they passed a pole with a flat board nailed to it. On it was the word 'WARBONNET.' burned into the wood with a red-hot iron. Some fancy-shooting man had added a full-stop with a slug from a .45 and holed the O dead centre.

They rode on, silent now, partly with

tiredness, partly with the constraint laid on them by new surroundings, new conditions. The trail into town was worn and rutted with wagon-wheels and the hooves of cows and horses.

'There's close on two thousand people in this town,' said Dayton.

'I expect I shall enjoy being there tomorrow,' she said primly.

When they were still some way out the town began to make its presence heard. At first it was no more than a faint susurrus of noise and then as they rode closer it deepened into a steady muted roar. She turned her face inquiringly towards him and aware of it he answered the unspoken question.

'Friday night,' he said. 'They've poured in there all day, soldiers, miners, cowhands, drifters, even the roughnecks from the badlands, bucking the faro and keno games, drinking, fighting.'

'It sounds like a mighty rough town,' she said, a little timidly.

'It's rough,' he said. 'Rougher than anything you've ever seen.' He paused, his head bent slightly forward towards the town like a gun-dog pointing.

'You'd do well to keep to your room. You'll be all right then.'

They were passing through the outskirts of the town now. Shacks and shanties crowded the edge of the trail and here and there lamp light laid its yellow path across the ruts of the road. There was a slight bend and as they rounded it they found themselves in the full flare and glare of naphtha lights. Noise surged and rocketed around them and the high cries of men excited by drink, women and the lusts of night. Minty kneed her pony close to Dayton's big bay. Stirrup to stirrup they rode on into the bright flaring street with its tinkling pianos, flapping batwing doors, lurching drunks. Twice in seconds they heard the hard flat roar of a gun.

'We turn off here,' Dayton said, as they reached an intersection. The road angling off to the left was quieter but not much. There were more stores and fewer saloons and then about twenty-five yards from the turning Dayton pulled up outside a big brightly-lit hotel. Looking up, Minty could see the name 'The Drovers' Hotel' painted in large black letters on a board stretching across the entire hotel frontage. It all looked raw and new and – in a way – exciting.

'We'll leave the horses here,' said Dayton, dismounting at the hitch-rack outside the hotel's main entrance. They tied their reins to the rail and after collecting their bed-rolls walked into the lamp-lit hotel lobby.

A reception clerk stood behind a desk. He was thin and pale. Long drooping moustaches made him look sadder and older than he probably was, thought Minty.

'We would like two rooms,' said Dayton quietly.

'There's only 21 an' 22 on the top floor,' said the clerk huskily.

He stared at Minty briefly with empty grey eyes and then added, 'Still, they're adjoining, mister.'

Dayton said, 'It wouldn't matter if they were the width of the hotel apart.' The clerk said, 'No, sir,' hurriedly and turned to the key-board behind him. Minty stood still, admiring the large chandelier hanging in a room to the left of the desk. From beyond came the tinkling of a piano, laughter, the clink of glasses, the loud hum of animated conversation. She felt an enormous longing to take one peep into it.

'If you'll just sign here, ma'am,' the hotel clerk was saying.

She turned to the desk and signed her name slowly and a little awkwardly in the space indicated by the clerk. As she wrote she registered the words William Dayton in

strong bold letters above her own. Bridgerville she wrote too as he had done and then
she put the pen down and looked at Dayton
towering above her. Always she thought,
with that strange, half-angry look in his eyes.

'The dining-room is on your right,' said
the clerk.

'Reckon you'd like to clean up,' Dayton
said to her. 'Then we can eat.'

She said, 'Thank you,' and they walked
away to the staircase. She was aware as she
moved of the clerk's pale eyes following her.
Her levis seemed to shrink even tighter
around her hips and she longed to run.

Eventually they reached the top floor of
the hotel and the two rooms they had taken.
Dayton put the key in the lock of 21, turned
it and opened the door.

'I'll meet you down in the dining-room,'
he said. 'In about ten minutes,' she
promised and then almost hurriedly she
brushed past him and closed the door. He
went to his own room and washed the trail
dust out of his eyes and nose and hair. He
was aware now only of an impatient fine-
drawn hunger and when he had changed his
shirt and reknotted his scarf and combed
his hair he was ready. Instead of going out
however he sat on the bed, brass-knobbed

130

and pink-valanced and rolled himself a
cigarette. He allowed his mind to play back
over the last four days. Apart from the death
of Cimarron they had had luck. They had
ridden out a storm and a stampede. They'd
eluded the hostiles and now everything
depended on Seth Morum. He'd have to see
him. Maybe tonight. Have him out to look
over the cattle early next day.

He got up and went out into the corridor.
There was no sign of Minty and he went on
downstairs. In the foyer he hesitated. There
was probably time for a drink. He turned
right and through a door into a long bar. It
was beginning to fill up and a pianist at the
far end was working hard on a Stephen
Foster song.

Dayton went up to the bar, his slow deliberate movements, his big frame and his travel-
stained garb drawing the attention of the folk
already there. Most of them were towns-
people, some wearing custom store clothes
with here and there a cattleman in the range
garb of the Territory. The bartender moved
along the bar, his eye faintly supercilious.

'You lookin' for someone, mister?' he said.

'Not someone, something,' said Dayton
equably. 'Whisky, please.' The bartender
looked as if he were about to speak but there

131

was some indefinable quality in the big man looking at him that made him change his mind. He swept a cloth circular-wise over the polished mahogany bar-top, bent down and brought up a whisky bottle and a shot-glass.

Dayton took a silver dollar from his vest pocket and laid it on the counter. He filled the glass and then poured it down in one gulp. He stood quite still, staring now into the big ornate gilt mirror, savouring the dry smoky taste of the whisky, feeling its warmth spread out in him. It was a moment to enjoy at the end of four tough days and even as he stood there he was aware that he was now thrown back more and more on the pleasures of each isolated moment. He poured himself a second glass and was about to raise it to his lips when he heard the light step behind him.

It was Minty Toween. She had changed out of the boyish levis and shirt she had worn along the trail and was now wearing the blue cotton dress he'd last seen when they had first come to her grandfather's ranch.

She spoke quietly and was faintly flushed, 'I hope you don't mind, Will. I couldn't find you in the dining-room and I got kinda scairt.'

She was like a child in her plain little blue

dress and he was suddenly strongly affected by her simplicity.

Leaving his drink untasted he took her by the arm and said, 'Let's go eat, Minty. I'm that hungry I could eat a bull-buffalo, horns, hide an' all.'

She looked up at him, laughing. She was supremely happy and remained so while they ordered their meal and ate it. Occasionally while working on the large steak they bought her, she paused to admire the white napery of the table at which they sat or the mirrored walls.

'It's all very grand, isn't it, Will?' she said.

'Why, yes,' he said. 'Towns like Warbonnet are sure beginning to get civilised. One day they'll be like Chicago, with hundreds of hotels and stores an' folk driving around in their carriages.' He picked up his fork and knife. 'Ain't sure that that's a good thing, after all,' he said, staring down at his plate. 'Reckon I'm a happier man when I'm out in the hills than I am in town. Why, last time I was in Omaha...'

He stopped short, suddenly, painfully aware of why he had last visited the big town in eastern Nebraska.

'Yes,' she prompted him, 'What happened then?'

'I buried my wife there,' he said, brutally.

It was the end of the evening for them both. Once the words were out he was aware of how cruelly he had embarrassed her. He had not meant to. The words had somehow slipped out. Covertly he watched her make a pretence of eating the apple pie in front of her. With not more than half of it eaten she gave up.

She put down the spoon she was holding and suddenly looked across the table at him. She said, 'I sure am sorry, Will Dayton. Reckon I knew you were grieved over something. But I didn't know it was that bad.'

'I didn't mean to bring it up,' he said in half-apology.

'Maybe it's better so.' Her eyes shone with sympathy. But once again he could not respond.

Words would not come. He got up at last.

'If you'll excuse me I figure I'd better go find Seth Morum an' persuade him to buy your cows.'

She was glad of the chance to escape.

They walked out of the dining-room. At the foot of the stairs she put a small brown hand on his arm.

'I sure am mighty obliged to you, Will Dayton.'

He suddenly smiled again and humour relaxed his hard strong features into something pleasing and gentle that she had only occasionally glimpsed.

He said, 'I'll get things fixed overnight if Morum'll buy the cows without seeing 'em. If not I'll have to ride out early and show him what we've got.'

'I'll wait for you here,' she said and turned away. He watched her to the bend in the staircase where she turned and called down, 'Good-night.' As she climbed the second flight out of his sight she thumped the banisters with her fist saying furiously as she did so: 'I'd wait for you, Will Dayton, till Hell froze over.'

He went over to the reception desk and said to the clerk, 'Where'll I find Seth Morum at this time of night?'

'Mr Morum's habits are well known to me, Mr Dayton,' said the clerk primly.

He pulled a large repeater watch from his vest pocket, and consulted it. 'It is his custom at eight in the evening to play faro in The Longhorn Palace. At nine he is usually to be found in The Cattleman's Pride. It is now a half after eight and I think you can be sure of finding him in the first named.'

Dayton said, 'Thanks,' and went out into

the street. He walked up to the intersection and then angled across the main thorough-fare to The Longhorn Palace, a saloon and gambling hall that had flourished like the green bay tree of the saying since the early days when Warbonnet had been a roaring railhead town on the U.P trail.

It was still roaring but not with the ferocity of 1868 when the night sky seemed to pale under the yelling drunken impact of the railroad gangs. They had gone now but the miners, cowhands, gambling men and fancy women had taken their place. Dayton paused outside the big saloon, suddenly aware of an unaccountable tension in his muscles. And then he grinned to himself in the darkness. This was what remained in him of the long years of conflict. This was how he had felt when called upon to round up a gang of celebrating Paddies and bring them back into line. And now things were dif-ferent. He was for the moment a cattleman, or at any rate a cattlewoman's ramrod look-ing for a cattle buyer. He walked forward and pushed through the batwing doors.

Inside the saloon the air was thick with a blue haze of tobacco smoke, ringing with the strident voices of men. Through the heavy curtain of noise and smell the notes of a piano beat out a lively dance rhythm. Will Dayton could dimly make out at the far end of the long room a small stage on which four girls were performing a high-kicking dance act. To his left a bar ran down towards the stage. Men stood two-three deep along it, making the three housemen sweat with their clamorous demands. The gaming tables were over to his right and there he hoped to find Seth Morum.

It did not take long. Seth Morum was at the faro lay-out as the hotel clerk had said. Will Dayton watched him for a moment. A short stout man florid of face, wearing a brown Derby tilted backwards, his moustache a rich brown luxurious affair, his eyes small and calculating, the eyes of a shrewd business man.

When at last Dayton leaned forward and whispered, 'How's the cattle business?' he did not even turn his head.

'Things are bad, friend Dayton,' he said. 'Very bad.'

Dayton laughed.

'I've three hundred prime steers on a bed-ground just out of town, Seth.'

This time Morum put his cards down.

'I'm leaving the game for five minutes, Mr Bucket,' he said to the dealer.

Then he turned to Dayton. 'I figure we had better have a drink.'

They made their way across the crowded bar-room. They edged a way in among the drinkers and Morum wagged an imperious finger at one of the housemen.

'Whisky,' he said. He looked at Dayton appraisingly. 'You're thinner than you were, son.'

'Yes,' said Dayton.

'Three hundred steers you said. All gaunted up from the trail, I'll bet.'

'They're O.K.' said Dayton.

'Twenty dollars a head an' that's because you're a friend.'

'Twenty-five.'

'Be reasonable, Will. The market for beef ain't what it was.'

'There's the reservations and the army posts, not to mention the folks pouring in from the East,' continued Dayton.

Morum stared at him lengthily and then seemed satisfied with what he saw.

'Twenty-five it is,' he said. 'You drive a hard bargain, Will.' He reached into his inside pocket, 'You can have my cheque now. I'll send my boys for the cattle in the morning.' He obtained ink and a pen from the barman and wrote out a cheque for 7,500 dollars.

Dayton made out a bill of sale on an envelope that Morum provided. As Morum took it from Dayton he said, 'Didn't know you'd gone in for cattle-raisin', Will.'

'Haven't, as yet, Seth. This money's Miss Toween's, not mine.' Morum's eyes were bright with ill-suppressed curiosity but he managed to hold it in.

'I'll be returning to my game now,' he said and held out a plump hand. 'If you go in for the cattle-business, Will, I'm always at your service.'

They shook hands and Dayton turned to the bar for his drink. It was as he lifted it to his mouth that he looked accidentally in the big mirror behind the bar and saw the hard eyes and unshaven chin of a face he knew. It was Jed Moss, ramrod of the Toller crew, the man he'd pistol-whipped in the saloon at Bridgerville. Dayton did not think it was mere coincidence.

He continued the arrested movement of his hand, swallowing the rest of the whisky in one draught. He thought fast, knowing that this was no moment for trouble. Not till he got the cheque to the girl. When that was done he could turn to Moss. He waited, wholly tense. But nothing happened. Slowly he pivoted towards the part of the saloon where the Toller man should be standing, but he had gone.

As he felt the tension drain out of him he was conscious of an immense bone-deep weariness.

He slowly made his way through the drinkers and card-players towards the door of the saloon. He would give the girl her cheque, see she got it safely cashed in the morning and then ... and then... He shouldered his way out through the batwing doors into the darkness of the main street of the town. The noise and bustle had gone, was all concentrated inside the saloons and honky-tonks and bawdy houses of this lusty frontier town. A hundred yards away a solitary drunk wove an unsteady track through a pool of yellow lamplight streaming out from the window of a store. Dayton started to walk towards the intersection and then hesitated. There was something wrong. A premonition of danger laid its tiny chill hand on his nerves and slowly his right hand went down to the gun-belt at his hip. It was then that a gun flamed and boomed not thirty yards from where he stood. The bullet smashed its way into the wall of the saloon. Immediately another gun opened up from across the street and the window just to his left smashed splintering inwards. Dayton drew and fired twice rapidly at the point from which the first shot had come. Two shots came back at him, a third from across the street. A pure flame of anger seemed then to pass through him and he suddenly ran out ducking low, zig-zagging across the open space firing as he ran. There was one final shot from his second assailant and then he saw a dark figure detach itself from the shadow of a doorway and run awkwardly along the boardwalk. Dayton stopped in his tracks, took careful aim and fired. The man halted, cried out suddenly, swung round, and then seemed to catch at the wooden railing of the walk and sink slowly to the ground. Dayton waited for the first gun to start again but there was only silence now.

He walked cautiously towards the crumpled figure on the boardwalk. He was still holding his gun in his hand. He came closer, could see the ugly sprawl of the man he had shot. It was no sham. He drew near, bent down and struck a match to look at the white upturned face. It was that of a complete stranger, a pointed wolfish face once perhaps frightening, now merely surprised by death.

Other men were approaching and Dayton

straightened up to meet them. Light shone momentarily on a pointed star on a vest.

As they stood there he said slowly, 'My name's Dayton. This man and another tried to kill me as I came out of the Palace. I got this one. The other's made tracks.'

The man with a star knelt down and like Dayton struck a match. 'It's Dutch Ivens,' he announced and stood up. 'I'm Ed Lomas. You won't know me, mister, but I know you. You're trouble-shooter for the U.P railroad and you was here in '69 when the railroad first came thru'. I was drivin' stage outa here to Julesberg.' He looked down at the dead man. 'There won't be many folks a-grievin' over Dutch. He was just a cheap gunslinger who'd hev slit his own grandma's throat to git the gold out of her teeth.'

'It would be interesting to know who hired him this time,' said Dayton.

'Yes,' said the marshal. 'It sure would.'

'I'll be in town a couple of days if you want me,' said Dayton.

'Nothin' much to want you for,' said the marshall. 'Onless the folks decide to give you a medal for what you've done.'

Dayton said, 'Night,' and walked away towards the road leading to the Drovers. There would be no more trouble for the moment he thought. The other man he'd recognised in the saloon, had disappeared. He would give the girl her cheque in the morning but now he would sleep.

CHAPTER NINE

By nine o'clock next morning Minty had slept off the saddle-weariness of the past four days. She woke bright-eyed to the mounting clamour of the street outside the hotel. The novelty of everything was tempered only by the memory, still green, of her grandfather's death, but even this faded as she placed herself fully amid the excitement of all that the day was to be.

She slipped out of bed, filled the wash-basin with cold water and doused her face in it. It was only as she was drying herself that she saw the small note that had been pushed under her door. She walked across to pick it up half afraid now that something might come and spoil her new-found world of happiness.

The note said, 'The cattle are sold to Seth Morum. I have the cheque and will give it to you tomorrow. Yrs. Will Dayton.'

The handwriting she observed with a faint sense of pleasure was large and bold. She put the note on the dressing-table. She dressed automatically, her eyes on the small square of paper. It was the first letter she'd ever had from a man. Come to think of it, it was the first letter she'd ever had at all. She folded the note and tucked it carefully inside the neck of her dress. She suddenly saw herself in the tall mirror of the wardrobe. The blue cotton dress looked a mite rumpled and not at all like the modish gowns she had seen the night before in the hotel dining-room. A sense of hopelessness seized her and then suddenly she remembered the sale of the cattle. She had money now. She could buy any dress she wanted. She would buy the best dress in Warbonnet and surprise Will Dayton with it. She'd wear it to dinner that very night.

She went downstairs. In the lobby the hotel clerk eyed her and then said, 'Good morning,' without much enthusiasm.

She said, 'Good morning. Have you seen Mr Dayton?'

'Yes, madam,' said the clerk. 'Mr Dayton was up at seven o'clock. He told me to tell you that he'd be back here to meet you soon after nine.'

She glanced at the clock above the desk. It was a quarter after nine.

'I'll be having my breakfast,' she said. 'If

Mr Dayton comes, maybe you could tell him that I'm in the dining room.'

'I will do that,' said the clerk.

She entered the large dining-room. No-one was having breakfast. A tired-looking waitress took her order and she settled down to wait for Will Dayton. It was as she began on her second cup of coffee that she heard his voice out in the foyer.

Almost immediately he came in and sat at her table.

'Good morning,' said Minty. 'Would you like some coffee?'

'I sure would,' he said. 'I've been out to the bed-ground with Morum's hands. Ep Rollins rode back with me. He's stabling his horse. He'll be along in a few minutes.'

He took the cup she offered him and drank thirstily. He seemed to remember something suddenly for he put the cup down and reached into an inner pocket. His hand came out holding a pocket-book. From it he took out a folded paper which he passed to her. She opened it and sat staring wide-eyed at the figures on the cheque.

'Seven thousand five hundred dollars,' she whispered. 'Oh, Will, what a lot of money!'

'It's all yours,' he said smiling.

'Not all,' she replied firmly. 'Some of it's

yours and some's Ep Rollins'.'

'Not mine. You can pay off Rollins. He needs the money.' He sounded strangely abrupt, almost angry.

'I hired you,' she said. 'There's money owin' to you.'

'I came for the ride,' he said obstinately.

She was glaring angrily at him and about to say more when she was interrupted by Ep Rollins entering the dining-room. He looked tired, tousled, wild-eyed.

They stood up.

Minty said, 'Coffee, Ep?'

'I et an' drank all that was left at sun-up,' he said. 'I need two-three shots of red-eye an' then I'll hit the trail to the hills.'

'You'll be stickin' your neck out if you stay overlong in Warbonnet,' commented Dayton.

'Two-three drinks. That's all I ask.' Rollins grinned obstinately.

'I owe you money,' said Minty. She looked at the cheque she was still holding. 'Let's go along an' turn this into cash.'

They followed her out into the bright April morning and sauntered tall on each side on her to the bank which stood on Main. They were made welcome by the cashier, a thin, pallid man with quick nervous hands. He looked at the cheque which Minty offered

147

him and then asked what she wanted to do about the money.

'Grandpaw always said to put your money in a belt an' keep it with you,' she said, looking at Dayton.

'Could be a risk in carrying all that around with you,' said Dayton. 'Your best plan is to leave the money here an' pay off the note with a cheque which you can hand to the bank in Bridgerville.'

She stared at him for a few moments, her mind unaccustomed to dealing with the larger issues of money. Then reassured she turned to the cashier.

'I'll take five hundred dollars in cash,' she said. 'I'll also need a cheque to give to the bank in Bridgerville.'

'Yes, ma'am,' said the cashier. The formalities did not take long. Minty was given a receipt for her money, a cheque-book and five hundred dollars in a big envelope.

They left the bank. Outside on the boardwalk she dug into the envelope and drew out a sheaf of twenty dollar bills. She removed ten of them and held them out to Ep Rollins.

'That's two hundred dollars for your help,' she said. 'I hope it's fair.'

'It's too much, Miss Minty,' said Rollins.

148

The colour mounted rapidly to her cheeks.

She said, 'If you say one more word, Ep Rollins, I'll scream right here in front of the whole town.' She pushed the money at him and he took it, mumbling something about it being more than he deserved. However as if realising that it was useless to argue the point, he tucked the bills away in a pocket. Then he held out a hand first to Minty, then to Dayton.

'I'll be on my way now, folks. I aim to have my two-three drinks and then I'll mosey on. Ain't never liked towns overmuch and I reckon towns don't like me.'

He turned and made off along the board-walk. They watched him in silence cut across the rutted main street towards the Longhorn saloon.

'I'd sure feel easier if he'd ridden out of town,' said Dayton. Then he seemed to dismiss the vague worry about Ep Rollins and turned his attention to the girl at his side.

'There's still the question of money owin' to you, Will Dayton,' she said.

He looked down at her and then said quietly, 'I've got no pressin' need for money, Minty. Let's say, once again, that I came for the ride and that it was a pleasure to help.'

'A real pleasure?'

'Yes,' he said, his eyes giving back to hers the warmth of understanding. 'Yes, Minty, it sure was a real pleasure.'

'Then I'll never speak of the money again,' she said. 'Tomorrow I'll go back to Bridgerville an' pay off Grandpaw's note.' She looked up at him hesitantly. 'Then I figure to buy some more cattle an' start again.'

'Yes,' he said dubiously, dragging the word out so that she was immediately aware of his lack of enthusiasm.

'If you'd help me hire a couple of good men, Will, it wouldn't be difficult.'

'No,' he said. 'Mebbe so.' And then switching abruptly, 'How do you aim to get back to Bridgerville?'

'By train tomorrow,' she said. 'What'll I do about my pony?'

'I'll bring it back,' he offered.

'You'll be coming back. Why that sure is somethin' to look forward to.'

She was silent a moment, trying to summon up enough courage to say what she had to say. The words came with a rush.

'Will you be having dinner in the hotel tonight, Will?'

'Why, sure,' he said. 'Round about six o'clock, I reckon.'

'I'd like to have dinner with you, Will – that is, if I won't be takin' up your time.'

'Minty,' he said, 'I was countin' on it.'

Her smile at his words seemed to light up her whole being and looking at her Will Dayton realised that she was beautiful.

She said, 'I'm goin' to do some shoppin' but I'll be there by six o'clock.'

He said, 'So-long, Minty. Till six o'clock,' and strolled off up the long main street of the town.

She watched him as he walked away, seeing in him everything that she had ever dreamed of. Strong, big, capable and gentle too as her grandpaw had been. But so overshadowed by the past, by the woman he had been married to and who had died. Standing there in the sunshine she felt a pang of jealousy at the thought of another who had possessed him and still possessed him. And then she dismissed the thought as an unworthy one.

It was time to think about the dress she was going to buy and swiftly she realised that she had no idea how she was going to set about it. The idea of the dress and the desire to wear it that night when she had dinner with Will Dayton had suddenly become all-consuming. For a moment she was panic-stricken. And then she remembered the bank-cashier. He would know either of a shop or a dress-maker. She turned and re-entered the bank.

The cashier was behind his grille. He looked mildly surprised at seeing her again.

'Yes, Miss Toween,' he said. 'What can I do for you?'

'A small favour, mister. I want to buy a dress but I don't know where to go. I thought maybe you would know.'

The cashier considered the matter. Minty noted that he helped himself to think by rubbing his bald pate with the blunt end of a pencil.

'I doubt,' he said at last, 'that you'll find an emporium that provides ready-made gowns for ladies in Warbonnet, ma'am. There is however a dressmaker who might be able to help you.'

'I could try, couldn't I?' she said eagerly.

'No harm ever came of trying, ma'am. The dressmaker's name is Miss Amy Purcell. Her establishment is in the street that goes off at right-angles from Main about a hundred yards past the bank and quite near Harben's Dry Goods Store.'

She thanked him and hurried out. Anxiety about the dress made her half-run in the direction the cashier had indicated and she did not see the two men standing near the tie-rail of the Alamo Saloon, nor did she hear the taller man, Jed Moss, say to his companion. 'That's the girl, Cal. Don't lose touch with her from here on.'

'No, sir,' said the man called Cal and set out at once along the board-walk after the girl.

She reached Harben's Dry Goods store and the narrow street leading down from it very soon. About fifty yards from the corner she found herself standing outside a picket-fence surrounding a small house. On the gate were the words 'Miss Amy Purcell – Dressmaker.'

Minty went through the gate and knocked on the front door. It opened almost at once by a tall severe-looking woman who said, 'Yes?'

'I – I've come to see about a dress,' said Minty.

'In that case perhaps you'd better come in,' said the woman, ungraciously.

She led the way into a parlour and indicated a chair.

'I'm busy with a very important customer, Miss Belle Macquart, at the moment. However if you ain't pressed for time I may be able to attend to you in about fifteen minutes.'

'I ain't pressed,' said Minty. 'I'll wait right here.'

She waited, occupying herself for some time studying Miss Purcell's fading family portraits and her collection of pampas-grass, shells, small china ornaments and other bric-a-brac. She decided that the room was a little too overcrowded for comfort.

After what seemed a long time the door leading through to Miss Purcell's work-room opened and through it came the most elegant figure of a woman Minty had ever seen. She was fairly tall and lusciously curved. Her tight-fitting gown was a bright blue silk with a high necked lace collar and cuffs. She carried a reticule and a parasol. My, thought Minty, what a fashionable woman! She went out of the room saying to Miss Purcell, 'Send the bill to Mr Conroy at the Drovers.' In the doorway she turned and favoured Minty, with a bold scrutinizing stare and then surprisingly she winked and with a swirl of blue silk disappeared.

'Well,' said Miss Purcell, from the door-way, 'what can I do for you, Modom?'

'I want a red silk dress,' said Minty, and added hurriedly, 'Something like the one

154

the lady was wearing.'

'How soon do you want it?'

'Tonight,' said Minty as faintly as she could utter the word.

'Landsakes!' said Miss Purcell. 'It takes all of three weeks, with fittings, to make a dress like that. It would also be mighty expensive – about fifty dollars.'

'Oh!' said Minty, as the bottom fell out of her dream. 'The cost didn't matter.'

'Is it so all-fired important that you have the dress by tonight?' asked Miss Purcell, speaking more gently now than she had done hitherto.

'Yes,' said Minty. 'Yes, it was very important.'

Miss Purcell appeared to consider weightily for a moment.

'I've got a dress that might fit you,' she said at last. 'It was ordered by a young lady who had to – er – leave the town rather hurriedly.' Miss Purcell did not feel the need to add that the lady in question was Miss Polly Deloraine of the Eldorado Saloon on South Street or that she had been escorted to the East-bound train by Ed Lomas, the town marshal who had warned her never to return to Warbonnet.

They went into Miss Purcell's workroom

and the dress was produced from a large wardrobe. It was some apple-green material, heavy and faced with crimson.

Minty gasped as she saw it. 'Why it's a beautiful dress an' I reckon it's just about my size.'

Miss Purcell lost some of her rigidity and almost enthusiastically got down to the business of fitting her latest customer.

Ep Rollins crossed Main Street with the firm intention of having two drinks and two drinks only at the Longhorn Palace saloon before he got his horse and rode out of town. There were several other saloons before he came to the Longhorn and into each of them he went and had his first drink and in each one he spent a good long hour or more over his one drink, nursing it along much to the irritation of the bartender in each saloon he visited. He had no kind of liking for Warbonnet or its inhabitants, he decided as he left the Last Chance. Indeed, on one occasion some nine months back, he remembered it well, as he at last pushed open the batwing doors of the Longhorn Palace, he'd had to shoot his way out. The thought of that tight bitter moment came back to him now, as he walked a little unsteadily though the long empty room to the bar. It left him momentarily uncertain, hesitant and then he thought to hell with it. Six months in the hills without a drink was a mighty long time. A man could last so long but no longer.

A bartender came long the bar to meet him.

'Howdy,' said Ep Rollins.

'Mornin',' said the barman. He was a chunky-looking man with drooping moustaches and bleak grey eyes. 'Ain't I met you before some place?'

'Mebbe,' said Rollins. 'You must meet a lot of gents in your business.'

'That's so,' said the barman. 'What's your drink?'

'Whisky,' said Rollins. The barman had been there nine months before. Rollins didn't like him. The barman planked a bottle of Old Crow and a shot-glass in front of his customer. Rollins filled the glass and emptied it in one long swallow, the Adam's apple in his long thin neck bobbing up and down as he drank.

He put the glass down and breathed deeply.

'That sure hits the spot,' he said amiably. He pulled a sack of tobacco and papers from his vest pocket and proceeded to roll himself a cigarette. He finished it off with his left hand and with his right he refilled his glass. The barman watched him.

'Ain't no cause fer you to stand there an' watch me like a buzzard watching a pack-rat,' said Rollins. 'This is my second an' last drink an' I aim to finish it peacable-like.'

'I ain't no buzzard, mister,' said the barman, dropping both his hands below the level of the bartop. 'I'll trouble you to finish this last drink you're takin' an' get on out.'

Rollins raised his glass and once more drank the whisky in one long gulp. He put it down on the bar-top and as he did so his hand flashed down and came up holding a Colt's .45.

'An' I'll trouble you to put both your hands where I can see 'em, bartender. Easy now and then we can have a nice quiet little pow-wow together, jist like a coupla prairie dogs in a hole.'

The barman brought his hands up and rested them on the well-polished mahogany bar. His face had paled but his cold grey eyes glinted now with fury.

'Did I say this was my last drink?' said Rollins. 'If so, I was plumb wrong. I'm goin' to have another drink an' then another an' mebbe after that another.'

As if to prove his point, he filled his glass for the third time. His gun he returned to its holster. The barman continued to watch him balefully. Rollins sipped his drink and thought about the hills of Idaho and the tall timber. He'd built a thousand camp-fires up there and watched the western sky flare up and die away and seen the bright stars twinkle out.

'I'm hungry,' he said suddenly to the bartender. 'I'm as empty as one of last year's tomato cans. Where do I eat?'

'Not here,' said the bartender. He looked up anxiously at the clock on the bar.

It was a half after five. The people that mattered in Warbonnet would be in soon and here he was with this crazy man to deal with.

'I want a large steak, with fried potatoes,' announced Rollins.

'If you wanna eat,' said the bartender, 'you'll have to go someplace else. This ain't no restaurant.'

'I aim to eat,' said Rollins coldly. 'I don't live to eat an' I don't eat to live. I jest eat when my insides tell me to.' He drew his gun and waggled it suggestively. 'You jest mosey along and git me some vittles, Mr Bartender.'

'Nope,' said the bartender obstinately.

Men further along the bar took their glasses and moved away. Seth Morum coming in for an unusually early drink took in the situation in one rapid glance. The man with the gun was Ep Rollins who'd been with Will Dayton on the cattle drive. He heard Rollins say:

'Git up on the bartop, mister or I'll sure ventilate you.'

He saw the bartender climb up and stand on the bar.

'Dance,' said Rollins coldly. He fired once into the floor next the bar.

The barman began an ungainly shuffle on his polished mahogany bar. It was time to do something, Morum decided, before things got out of hand. He spotted one of his men at the table near the wall. He went over. 'Go. Get Will Dayton pronto,' he said. 'You'll probably find him at the Drovers.'

'Keep it goin,' yelled Ep Rollins. 'This is as good as a variety theatre.'

It took a long time before Miss Purcell was satisfied with the alterations needed for the dress but by a half after three the work was done. The grateful Minty dug into her wad of bills and paid the dressmaker twenty-five dollars. It wasn't such a lot of money when you looked at the dress, she decided. There was an hour's sewing to be done and Miss Purcell suggested that she should return for the dress at five o'clock.

'I will go shopping then,' said Minty and Miss Purcell saw her out. An hour went very quickly in the stores of Main Street and loaded down with new shoes, hairpins, ribbon and other purchases Minty returned at five o'clock, collected the dress and somehow managed to reach the hotel without dropping any of them. Her first act was to untie a small parcel and admire its contents. It was a pipe with a bright silver band – a very good pipe, the store-keeper assured her. It had come all the way from England and it had cost twelve dollars. It was for Will Dayton. She hoped it would be to his liking. There wasn't very much you could give a man and she well remembered her grandpaw's love for two old battered pipes. She parcelled the pipe afresh.

It was time now she knew to put on the new dress to get ready for the last night's dinner together. As she washed and changed her clothes she was aware of an ever-growing excitement. Looking in the mirror of the dressing-table she saw the flush in her cheeks, the brightness of her eyes. Slowly, with a deliberate enjoyment, she piled her hair high up onto her head, working the new hairpins into the neat structure of hair until at last she was satisfied with her newly sophisticated appearance. Then she took up the dress, working it up slowly around her hips, slipping her arms into the close-fitting sleeves, finally buttoning it up from the waist to the neck. Lastly she put on her daring two inch high-heeled shoes and knew that the moment had come. She picked up the present for Will Dayton. She had one final look in the mirror at the stranger she had become and then turning she crossed the room and went out into the corridor.

It was not very far to the stairhead but it seemed a mighty long way with so much new gear to handle. Slowly she made her way down, terrified that she might trip over the unfamiliar long skirt. She reached the foyer and saw the desk clerk gaping at her.

'Have you seen Mr Dayton?' she asked.

'Yes, ma'am,' said the clerk. 'Right in there, in the bar-room.'

She decided to go in and surprise him. She moved still tentatively towards the half-curtained entrance to the bar and pulling the curtains aside went in.

She saw Will Dayton almost at once.

Standing not more than a lariat's length away from her. He was talking animatedly to a woman. Minty stared. It was the woman who had walked out of Miss Purcell's, the one called Belle Macquart, and Will Dayton's hand was resting on her arm. She felt her face turn scarlet with mortification. It was then that Will Dayton's gaze shifted to her direction and she saw the fading smile around his mouth and eyes. Suddenly stricken Minty turned almost blindly away. She pushed her way through the curtains and half-ran through the foyer and upstairs to her room. As she stripped off the new dress and pulled on her old levis her mind was working furiously. What a goldarned fool to imagine that a man like Will Dayton would be interested in her, especially with folks like Belle Macquart to turn to. Her anger was directed not at him but at something in herself and now she knew only the furious need for action. She must get away now.

She snatched up the new dress and her old blue cotton, rammed them into her saddle-bag. In less than three minutes she was ready to go and then with her hand on the handle of the door she paused. What if it was all a mistake? If so he would be here by now with an explanation. But he had not come. Sufficient proof that dinner with Minty Toween meant nothing to him when he was in the company of Belle Macquart. She opened the door and hurried downstairs.

She said to the clerk, 'I'm leavin', how much do I owe?'

He consulted books and papers while she fidgeted to be away. She'd take her pony and ride back, following the railroad. She'd get back and make her own way.

'Eleven dollars and twenty cents, Miss Toween,' said the clerk.

She paid him and hurried out.

It was almost twilight already as she hurried along to the livery stable and she did not see the two men watching her from the shadow of an alley almost opposite the hotel. They followed her to the stable, waited until she had got her pony and then without speaking trailed her at a distance of a quarter of a mile as she rode out into the last glowing light of the western sky.

CHAPTER TEN

After parting with Minty Toween outside the Bank, Dayton had found himself at a loose end. He idled the morning away, ate a large meal at midday, slept until five o'clock and finally wandered downstairs into the bar room of the Drovers. He stood at the bar for five minutes, taking his first drink for the day slowly and appreciatively. But, behind the surface feeling of idle contentment with the moment's pleasure there was a growing awareness once more that he was no further forward than when he had got off the train at Bridgerville five-six days ago. In the whirling activity of getting Minty Toween's cattle to Warbonnet, in the stampede, the skirmish with the Indians, the gun battle of the previous night, his own problems had been set aside, forgotten. But now the restlessness was working like yeast in him again. He poured himself a second drink and absently rolled a cigarette. It was just as he raised a match to light it that a voice behind him said, 'Reach for the sky, pardner. I've got you covered.'

He turned slowly to find himself face to face with a woman he had not seen for three years.

'Why, Belle Macquart!' he said, 'It sure is good to see you again.'

She laughed richly and held out a hand.

'It's good to see you, Will Dayton. What a lot of water's gone under the bridge since you and I were in Julesberg.'

'That's a time we'd both do better to forget,' he observed gravely.

'I was young and foolish then,' she said, still smiling, for the big reserved dangerous man had always pleased her, even in the riotous days of Julesberg, when he and the wild Paddies working for him had torn down a whole saloon in less than an hour. Her saloon.

'Still young and still beautiful,' he said. 'What will you drink, Belle?'

'Whisky, please, Will.' The memory of how he'd walked into the Eldorado, had his drink with her, asked her briefly why one of his men had managed to get himself dry-gulched in the bedroom of one of her girls, and then, without batting an eyelid had called in the wrecking gang.

'Things were mighty wild in those days,'

she said. 'What have you been up to since then?'

'I've helped build another railroad,' he said. 'A small one, a spur line. I've been married.'

'Been married, Will?'

'Yea,' he said. 'My wife died two weeks ago.'

'I'm sorry,' she said, touching his arm lightly with her hand.

'Since then I've been in the cattle business again – briefly. My employer is due to have dinner with me tonight.' He told her about Minty Toween, of the trouble at the Toween ranch, of the drive through the Indian country and the gun-fight in the street of Warbonnet.

'How old is she?' said Belle Macquart.

'About eighteen, I reckon,' said Dayton. And then as if avoiding the topic he asked, 'What are you doing now, Belle?'

'Much the same as before, Will. I have a nice quiet house and six very well-behaved girls. My clients are all highly respectable citizens.'

He said, 'I ought to disapprove of you. I don't. Maybe it's because I'm not a highly respectable citizen.'

'I'm glad you're not,' she said and once

again touched the sleeve of his coat.

Something made Will Dayton turn his head towards the hotel entrance to the saloon and it was then that he saw Minty standing alone there, almost unrecognisable for a moment in an unfamiliar and beautiful green dress, unfamiliar too was the sadness of her expression. And then just as he was about to move across to her, she turned abruptly and fled. At the same moment a stranger came up to him and said,

'Mr Dayton, I've got a message for you. Seth Morum says to come quick over to the Longhorn and git Ep Rollins out of trouble.'

The words pulled him up short. The vision of the girl's distressed face was gone. Ep Rollins' words, 'I ain't popular in Warbonnet,' came back to him now with a full meaning in them. Rollins had come to Warbonnet to please him and it was up to him to see that Rollins got out of town with a whole skin.

'Be seeing you, Belle,' he said and hurried out of the Drovers' bar-room. Belle Macquart watched him go, not knowing quite why she felt as she did. Dayton strode towards the intersection and then across Main to the Longhorn. It was like other times, other places, he reflected a little grimly. A friend, an employee, a railroad man, trapped in some saloon or honky-tonk. Send for Will Dayton to shoot him free.

He hitched his gun-belt a fraction to the left and pushed his way through the swing-doors of the big salon. He summed up the situation in one rapid glance at the bar – with its crouching white-faced bartender atop, the ring of onlookers and leaning against the wall Ep Rollins, looking pale and a little wilder than usual. It was an old pattern of trouble, with violence rising like a tide in all of them there.

Standing there he heard a voice say, 'Throw your gun down, mister, an' we'll leave it at that.'

He heard Rollins laugh sardonically. 'I'll keep the gun. Reckon it's safer so.'

'Rush him, boys,' a voice yelled. 'He's too goddam drunk to shoot straight.'

It was true. Dayton moved fast, shouldering a brutal way through the close-packed line of the mob. Someone grabbed at his shoulder but he pulled away, forcing through by sheer animal strength. Rollins saw him coming and grinned like a death's-head.

Dayton turned towards the crowd and the rank scent of danger came from them.

'I'll take this man where he'll cause no more trouble,' he said, slowly. His only answer was a wild-dog growling from the crowd. They were fully ripe for trouble now. Anything would spark them off.

'We're getting out of here now,' he said briefly to Rollins.

'Lead on, Macduff,' came Rollins' reply.

'Back up to me,' said Dayton and drew his gun. He walked straight towards the crowd knowing that they were a crowd only, leaderless. He came full up against one man, putting him solely under the threat of the gun and the man went white and pulled back. Dayton moved fast into the gap, aware of Rollins close behind him. A white yelling face rose up before him, big hands grabbed wildly at his neck. He slashed the man a raking terrible blow with the gun-barrel and plunged out of the ring. He turned knowing now that he could and saw Rollins suddenly go down and feet kicking at him. Dayton fired once, the bullet smashing into the floorboards not a foot from Rollins' head. He ran forward, grabbed Rollins and heaved him to his feet, his gun alone holding off the mob.

'Out,' he yelled and fired again into the floorboards. He backed slowly, warily, towards the saloon entrance and suddenly felt the cooler air coming in behind him over the batwing doors. He heard Seth Morum's voice suddenly raised.

And then they were out and making for the livery stable.

'You'd better hightail it out of here fast,' Dayton said.

'Yep,' said Rollins breathing hard. 'Sure am sorry I got you into this ruckus, Will.'

Dayton grunted. 'What were you trying to prove, Ep?'

Rollins made no reply, lurching into the livery stable. It took him no more than a minute to get his horse saddled. He swung up at the entrance.

'There's a small matter of payment,' said the liveryman, irritably.

'The gent's in a hurry,' said Dayton. 'I'll settle his bill.'

'Thanks, Will,' said Rollins. 'Reckon I was tryin' to prove that you can't run away from things forever.' He grinned in the yellow light of the lantern.

'Mebbe I was a bit drunk, too. Mebbe I still am. Adios, Will.'

'So long, Ep,' said Dayton and stood watching Ep Rollins trot away into the darkness, back to the high hills.

Suddenly he laughed and the liveryman stared at him.

Dayton said, 'How much did he owe you?'

'Two dollars.' Seeing Dayton's stare he added lamely, 'Prices is high in Warbonnet, mister.'

Dayton paid him and walked slowly back to the hotel. He was still amused by Rollins' capacity for raising hell. But then Rollins had always been like that. And crowds always hated a lone wolf.

He turned the corner into the street where the Drovers stood. Two riders whirled past him heading out of town. Climbing the steps of the hotel entrance he paused, remembering Minty's expression as she stood in the doorway. He went on into the hotel, glanced into the dining-room. It was empty. He went into the bar-room. Belle Macquart was no longer there but the place was busy. Men lined the long bar, drinking, talking. He was suddenly aware of tiredness, now that the keyed-up excitement of the incident at the Longhorn was over. He went up to the bar and bought a drink. He built himself a cigarette. Five minutes to ease the tension out of himself and then he'd go on up and see why the girl hadn't come down. Maybe it had been some momentary fit of embarrassment. He drank slowly, vaguely irritated by his own lack of understanding where the feminine sex was concerned.

His drink finished, he made his way out and went upstairs. He went up to the door of her room and knocked gently. There was no reply and he knocked again – a little harder. He tried the handle of the door. It turned and he went in. On the threshold he paused, wondering whether she was asleep. He struck a match, saw the lamp on a table and lit it. He stood there while the yellow lamp-light slowly crept down the walls and showed an empty hotel room, with nothing at all to show that it had been used, occupied less than an hour ago. And then he saw a small packet on the floor near the dressing-table. He went over, picked it up, instantly know-ing by weight and shape that it was a pipe. Understanding slowly grew out of the con-fusion of objects and incidents and with it a deep-seated anxiety for her was a sudden leaden weight in him.

Turning he hurried out of the room and ran down the stairs.

'Have you seen Miss Toween?' he said to the clerk.

'Miss Toween? Why, yessir, about an hour ago. She paid her bill and left.'

173

'Where was she going?' Dayton's voice in his own ears was strained and harsh.

'She didn't say, Mr Dayton. Just paid her bill an' walked out. She took her saddle-bag and a large package.'

Dayton said 'Thanks' and walked out of the hotel. The livery-stable was the most likely place and there he hurried, heavy now with foreboding.

The liveryman was sitting just inside the big doors of his barn, nursing a bottle. He looked up incuriously at the big man approaching.

'Has Miss Toween been in to get her horse in the last hour?' said Dayton.

'Don't know any Miz Toween.' The man spat in the dust. 'Ain't my business to know all the folks in the town.'

Dayton put out a big hand, grabbed the man by the front of his shirt and jerked him to his feet.

'I haven't got any time for talk, mister. Has the girl been in for her pony or not?'

'She was in all of an hour gone, paid up an' rode off,' the man said sullenly.

'Which way did she go?'

'West,' said the liveryman.

There was only one thing to be done.

'Have my horse ready in ten minutes,' said

Dayton and strode off. He collected his saddle-bag and bed-roll from his room, paid his bill and returned. The bay was saddled up and ready. Dayton checked the cinches and girth. He tied his roll on behind the saddle and then asked for his bill.

'Two dollars,' said the liveryman sourly.

Dayton paid him and climbed into the saddle. He collected coffee, bacon and beans from a store and headed the pony slowly along the main street of Warbonnet, uncertain now of everything except the one firm resolve to catch up with Minty Toween before she rode into trouble.

At the edge of town after a match-lit search of the ground he found the fresh tracks of her pony in the sandy soil, heading, as the liveryman had rightly said, due west. He followed slowly, confident that he could catch up with her, feeling fairly certain that she would make camp for the night now that full darkness was closing down on the vast spaces of the prairie.

The trail was fairly well defined, running parallel with the railroad. After a time he knew it would have to branch off north to get round a hill that abutted on the railroad. It was here that he hoped to catch up with her. He rode doggedly on in the gathering darkness, the silence of the early night broken only by the quick cheeping of some frightened bird, a sudden rustle in a thicket or far off the hooting of an owl. In less than an hour he reached the hill, by which time the moon was well up and there was the slight advantage of its fine silvery radiance. But nothing showed. No camp-fire or grazing pony. Nothing.

CHAPTER ELEVEN

Minty rode out of town in the last light of afternoon feeling only a kind of numbness. All the excitement of the day, the visit to the dressmaker, the dress itself, the preparation for the dinner with Will Dayton, it had all dissolved now into a confused blur of unhappiness. She was aware only of a dreary hopelessness, a desert peopled only by herself. To think of Will Dayton pawing some painted woman like that; that Belle Macquart. It was maddening beyond words.

As her pony paced on she said aloud, 'I'll never speak to him again. Never! Never!' And for each 'never' she thumped the saddle-horn with a small clenched fist. The pony took this as an indication of some urgency and went off at a gallop which helped for a time to obscure the misery of her thoughts. Gradually it slowed to a canter and then to a gentle trot. Minty watched the last faint yellow patch of sky slowly grey over into night. It wakened her a little more fully to the world around her and to the folly of what she was

doing. She was alone now in the vast emptiness of the prairie with nothing for company
but wandering hostile Indians and coyotes
out hunting.

'Better than stay there to be shamed,' she
said aloud and patted the pony's neck.

She let it trot on and after a time she
realised that the trail was bending away from
the faint line of the railroad, leading, she sur-
mised around the heavy mass of a steep hill.
The hill and the valley through which she
was now riding was just faintly visible in the
fast-fading light. Over to her left a long ridge
stretched out from the hill. She rode on.
About a hundred yards farther on she
thought she heard a horse whinny. She reined
in listening, tense with a growing, unformed
fear. Again she rode on, resolved now to
camp at the first likely place she came to.

It was as she strained her eyes in the gloom
searching for a place to camp that she heard
the unmistakeable hoofbeats of horses, close
now and coming fast. She spurred her pony
suddenly into a dead run cutting away from
the trail. But they drew up on her and she
was aware of them no more than a few yards
behind. The drumming beat of the pursuing
horses grew louder and louder and then
suddenly she was aware of the two dark

shapes, one on each side of her, of a hand stretching out towards her. Then it grabbed the reins and she screamed. The pony came to a sudden stop and she was jolted forward against the saddle-horn, breathless, terrified.

'Git down, missy,' said a voice, quiet and smooth and deadly.

She did as she was told and standing found she could not stop her limbs shaking.

'You didn't oughter git spooked like that, missy. We don't aim to do you any harm.'

It was the same softly confident, terrifying voice that had spoken before. She tried to see the speaker through the darkness.

'What are you aimin' to do with me?' Her voice was as shaky as her legs, she realised.

'We're jest an escort as you might say. We're jest takin' you along to see someone who's kinda interested in you.'

'No one's that interested in me,' she said flatly.

'There's no tellin' what folks is interested in,' said her captor, mildly.

'Who is it?'

'That'll keep till later. We won't see him yet awhile.' He paused and there was the sudden spurt of a match, its yellow brilliance lighting up the speaker's face as he lit a cigarette. It was a face she knew, still quite young, but hard and cruel. The man's bleached blue eyes regarded her coldly through the match-light. Then it went out and she stood there waiting, in a kind of fatalistic numbness. It was the face of Jed Moss, the Toller's ramrod.

'Reckon we'll ride on now,' said the man. 'Maybe we'll make camp later when we know we ain't being followed.'

The other man spoke then for the first time. 'I'm plumb wore out, Jed. Why not bed down here for a coupla hours. No one's goin' to trail us.'

'Mebbe you've forgot a hombre by the name of Dayton,' said the man called Jed. 'Maybe you've forgot what happened last night back in town. It won't take him long to discover that the girl's missin', Cal, and then he'll be on her trail. Let's ride. I'll give the say-so when we're to make camp.'

He proceeded to tie a lead-rope to Minty's pony and thus linked they rode on through the long hours of night. At first they went straight up valley but after about an hour they reached higher ground and the leader's progress became a series of twists and turns through half-seen washes and small canyons. Finally they emerged on a wide moon-washed plateau. Jed Moss led the way unspeaking, inexorable. At last even he seemed to have had enough. As he reached a clump of cottonwoods he said, 'We'll camp here till first light.'

Minty dazed and weary slid out of the saddle. She took her bed-roll over to the base of one of the trees, wrapped the blanket around her and almost at once drifted off into a broken uneasy sleep. The two men after picketing the horses followed her example. Jed Moss had no fear now of anyone finding them. Even a blood-hound would have had difficulty in following his trail. Before turning in he went over and looked down at the sleeping girl. A part of her face was exposed to the light of the moon and looking at her he was filled with a sudden inexplicable sense of regret. He had been outside the law for a long time now. He had robbed and cheated and killed when necessary. But he had never hurt a woman, had never been mixed up with one. He wondered vaguely as he pulled his blanket around him whether he was not at last making the irrevocable mistake.

Minty slept uneasily on the hard ground and woke just as the first grey light lifted on the prairie. She lay staring for a moment at a tree and a great rock slowly growing blacker and more definite before her. The whole nightmare of her capture came back and she sat up hastily, to find herself looking into the cold eyes of Jed. He was hunkered down over a small fire building it up hot enough to make coffee.

'By rights,' he said, watching her, 'you oughter be doin' this, missy.' She did not answer him feeling there was nothing to be gained from talking to either of them. Her one hope lay in escape. She stared around her, at the still blanket-wrapped form of the other man, the horses grazing about twenty yards off and the fall of the ground away to the west of their camp.

'You wouldn't be figuring on how to make a run for it, now, would you?' He seemed to have some uncanny gift for reading her thoughts. She shrugged and said nothing.

They had coffee, bacon and beans and then once more rode on. On and on and on through the warming sunlight, on through the heat of afternoon. They crossed a high range of hills and came down into a great wide valley. It looked like the valley of the Montana trail she had crossed with Dayton and Rollins and Cimarron only a few days back.

They reached the foothills on the far side

by late afternoon and here it was that, while breathing their mounts on a ridge top after a climb, they saw way down below them a file of riders moving south, raising a fine small plume of dust in their wake. The riders must have seen them for they stopped and there was a series of flashes of sunlight on glass or metal.

Jed Moss watched them narrowly, tightening his grip on the lead-rope of Minty's pony.

'Soldierboys,' he said contemptuously. 'Checkin' up on us with their spy-glasses.'

'Reckon we'd better move on fast,' said the one named Cal, anxiously.

'They won't come a-chasin' after us,' said Moss. 'They're only interested in one thing and that's Injuns.'

But Minty noticed that he pressed on hard and only seemed to relax when they had put another twenty miles of hill-country between them and the cavalry patrol.

They stopped at last and made camp in a canyon through which a small stream ran. After supper which was a repetition of breakfast the two men lounged near the fire. Minty had been aware of being watched by the man called Cal for some time and something inside her went cold now as he suddenly got up and came over to her.

He sat close to her and she felt herself go rigid with fear.

'How about a li'l old kiss for li'l old Cal,' he whispered.

Minty looked across at Moss, wondering painfully if he would intervene. But he only sat still watching them with cold bleak eyes. Cal put his arm around her shoulders and pulled her down flat on the ground. He leaned over her holding her shoulders with his hands. Minty stared up in horror at his thin cruel mouth, his unshaven face and small feral eyes. He bent lower while her body heaved and struggled in vain.

'You're jest about the right size for a roll in the hay,' he said and clamped his mouth down on hers.

She was aware briefly of the hideousness of his embrace and then suddenly it was gone. There was a confused struggle above her and then the short hard thud of a fist on flesh. She half-rose and saw her attacker reel back as Moss smashed a left and a right to the man's face. And then he was down and she heard Jed say, 'Don't lay a finger on the girl, d'you hear? Try it again an' I'll shoot your hands off.' Then he came over towards her, breathing hard, menacing in the faint light.

'Don't git any ideas, missy. I'm jest a-carryin' out the boss's orders, see.'

Then he turned away and she was left shaking and appalled, to wait, sleeping only fitfully, for the dawn of another day.

It came after hours of broken restless fear-ridden sleep, the thinning of the darkness, the first twittering of the dawn chorus of birds, the chill seeming to grow as she sat up. They breakfasted in a sullen silence, mounted on their horses and rode out before the sun was up.

Four hours of riding later and she knew where she was. They were on Toller land now and the approaching bulk of the Twin Buttes gave her an idea of their position.

They went on steadily westwards and she knew as they rode under the Buttes that they were not heading for the Toller ranch.

The long hours in the saddle, the only scanty supply of food were now joined by a chill sense of foreboding. She felt herself sway in the saddle and half angrily pulled herself erect. She must not give in now. Hold on and something would happen to save her. She thought half feverishly of Will Dayton. What had he done when he had discovered that she had gone?

Light softened as they rode on, slowly

now, on a fairly steep up-grade. And then not very far ahead in the shelter of a clump of pines she saw the vague outline of a shack. A line-camp she guessed. Moss rode straight towards it. As they approached a door opened and a man came out to meet them. At first he was only a dark figure and then as they drew near she began to see him more clearly and then within ten yards she saw that her worst fears had been realised.

It was Brad Toller who stood there grinning complacently at them. His eyes were on her, Minty saw but he addressed himself to Jed Moss.

'There's time for a bite and some coffee,' he said. 'Then we saddle up and ride up to Nugget.' He grinned again. 'He's waitin' there with a bottle for company.'

Moss climbed out of his saddle. Brad Toller came over to where she sat her pony. 'You can get off that pony,' he said.

She slid down to earth, sick now with fear.

He said, 'Go on in the shack. Maybe I'll give you some coffee if you're a good girl.'

She walked past him half-unseeing and stumbled at the threshold. An arm came out and steadied her.

'You're nigh to being tuckered out, missy,' said Jed Moss. 'You go sit on that box an' I'll bring you some cawfee.'

Even in her confusion and fear and wretchedness she knew that under the harsh voice there was some kind of consideration, some touch of feeling. She sat down on the old box and stared at the room with its litter of tins, scraps of paper, a rickety table. A blackened coffee-pot steamed over a fire and from this Jed Moss fetched her a mug of black coffee. It was hot and strong. She drank it gratefully and felt some of the weariness and tenseness ease out of her. And then Brad Toller came in, bulking large and dominant in the doorway.

Minty stared at him and at last found the courage to speak.

'Where – where are you taking me?'

Brad Toller laughed, a hard ugly sound.

'Why, I'm taking you to a preacher, girl, to get hitched.'

'Hitched!'

'Married. Married to me. Ain't that fine an' dandy now?'

'Married!' she breathed. 'I'll never marry you. I'd sooner marry a horned toad.'

'Kinda uppity, ain't you, Miss Toween.' He came lazily over towards her. He bent towards her saying, 'We'll have to see about tamin' you some,' and then he batted the mug of coffee out of her trembling hand. He followed this with a blow on her cheek that made her reel sideways off the box. She was aware then that he had been pulled up short and swung around.

'Ain't no call to treat the lady like a wild hoss,' said the strange grating voice of Jed Moss.

'Are you aimin' to horn in on my private business, Jed?' said Toller, softly.

'Maybe,' said Moss. 'Aint never taken to mistreatin' a lady.'

'Lady!' Toller laughed. 'This ain't no lady. She's just pore white an' there's only one way to deal with her kind – like this – an' this.'

As he finished he swung round and again smacked Minty's face with his hard open hand. There wasn't time for more. Jed Moss pulled him round a second time and drove a hard swinging right at his jaw. Toller went over like a pole-axed steer and lay flat on his back for a moment on the hard-packed earth floor of the cabin. Then he slowly raised his head and shoulders and in his eyes there was a moment's flash of insanity.

'You shouldn't have done that, Jed,' he said softly. 'You shouldn't have done it.'

Minty felt as if she saw the gun first. It was

in Toller's hand and she screamed then as it fired and the cabin seemed to rock with the detonations. She saw Moss reel back under the terrible impact of the bullet. He made one groping gesture towards his holstered gun and again Toller's gun roared from near floor level. The bullet spun Moss around and then he fell and lay wholly still. Through veils of gunsmoke Minty watched Brad Toller slowly get up from his position on the floor. He stood for a moment staring down at the prostrate body of Jed Moss. And then he laughed once, a short hard barking laugh.

'He shouldn't have horned in on my affairs,' he said, addressing no one in particular.

Minty watched him with horror. He said to the man called Cal: 'Leave him as he is. There's no time to dig a grave now. We're ridin' out of here in ten minutes. Come back when we've finished our business in Nugget.'

The man made no reply but he came over and dragged the slack empty body into a corner of the room.

'You can get ready as soon as you like,' said Toller to Minty. 'Mebbe you'll learn now that I ain't foolin' when I say I'm goin' to marry you.'

She stood up on trembling legs and slowly made her way out of the room. In the now fallen darkness she could not at first see her pony. Then suddenly as if sensing her presence it whickered over to her right. She went to it and climbed slowly, like an old woman, into the saddle. She sat there waiting to be told what to do. There was nothing left in her now, no courage with which to face the gigantic fear of the next few hours or days or years. And sitting there she wept bitterly.

CHAPTER TWELVE

Dayton dismounted to make sure that he was following the pony's track and then his quick eye saw the change in their imprint. The hoof-marks suddenly showed deep in the sandy trail and then abruptly angled off north of the trail, the deep indentations showing that she had suddenly urged the pony into a gallop. He followed them, on foot now, for over two hundred yards and then he knew the reason for the unexpected change of direction and speed. The prints of two other horses joined those of the girl's pony, coming in from the hillside above. Looking up he could see the dark ridges in the moonlight. There they would have waited. Moving on he came at last to the point where they had caught her. The tracks were confused here. The ground was cut up as if they had swung around, grabbed the reins from her, pulled her lunging frightened pony to a sliding stop. He could see it all and standing there in the empty moonlit valley he cursed them with a deep and terrible bitterness. As his passion spent itself he was suddenly conscious of being drained of all strength and remembered that he had not eaten since midday. There was nothing now to do but wait for daylight and get down then to the long and deadly business of tracking the kidnappers to whatever lair they had chosen to take the girl.

Will Dayton rolled out of his blanket in the pre-dawn darkness and stood for a moment in the chill air. He built a small fire and made himself coffee and fried bacon. At other times this would have been the first small pleasing ritual of the day but there was too much now on his mind and conscience to permit of any kind of pleasure. Minty Toween had done a mighty fool-headed thing in riding out alone into the darkness but that was over and done with. What mattered now was to get her out of the hands of whoever had kidnapped her. As he drank the remains of his coffee his eyes narrowed as he considered the possibility of the crime being the work of Brad Toller. It figured all right. Carry the girl off and steal the cash. That didn't make sense. Carry her off and force her to sign over the ranch to them or just keep her until it was too late to pay off the old man's debt. Something much bigger than Minty Toween or Will Dayton hovered over everything else. Man's lust for woman and gold was strong but he killed and died for water. There was only one place to go and that was the Toller ranch. There he would get his answer.

He saddled the bay and then took a look at the tracks. They told a pretty clear story. The two men had had their way and had ridden off almost due west with one man leading, and, to judge from the regular nature of the second set of imprints, with the girl's horse on a lead-rope. After that one careful inspection Dayton did not trouble to slow himself down by further tracking. He was now a hundred per cent certain that the men and the girl were headed for the Toller ranch and towards that point he now rode, not hurrying, but keeping the bay at a steady mile-eating trot. He made a halt once near a bunch of cottonwoods and drank thirstily from his canteen. Then he rode on down-hill until about two hours later he came to the wide stretch of the Montana trail.

Dayton had his long look here from the crest of the last ridge before descending. As far as the eye could see there was no break in the flat brown monotony of the valley. No raised dust to reveal the passing of riders – Indian or White. Slowly he put the bay down the slope and rode across the broad miles. By late afternoon he reached the foothills on the western side of the valley.

As he rode up the first gentle slopes he looked over to his right and saw the first and only signs of life he'd seen since the previous day. There was a small dust cloud about two miles up-valley from where he stood. He decided to get up above whoever it was and check on it. He pushed the bay on harder, gained a ridge top and dismounted on the further side. He slid out of the saddle and crawled back to wait for whoever was coming. The small cloud of dust gradually drew nearer. He could see now the dark shapes of men and horses and then when they were not more than a mile away he saw the flash of sunlight on metal, the dark blue tunics, the neat formation of about a dozen riders. An army patrol. It could be that they'd seen something of the fugitives. He went back to the bay, mounted and rode downhill to meet the soldiers.

The officer at their head halted them as Dayton rode up. And then there came a swift recognition. It was Brown from Fort Terrill.

'Howdy,' Dayton said, as he rode up.

'We choose some strange places to meet in, Will,' said Brown. 'Where are you heading for?'

'West,' said Dayton. 'Over to the Toller Ranch.' He paused, wondering. And then he added, 'Seen anything of a couple of riders and a girl on your way down valley?'

'Don't know about any girl,' said the lieutenant his eyes suddenly curious. 'We saw three riders about two hours back. They were up on a high ridge and we took a look at them with the glasses. They weren't Indians so we didn't do any more about it. It's Indians the Army's interested in at the moment.' He paused and looked hard at Dayton. 'Anything I can do?'

'No,' said Dayton. 'I can handle it.' He raised a hand in salutation swung the bay's head west and rode away.

'He certainly looks like he could handle most things, sir,' observed the troop sergeant, watching the retreating back of Dayton.

'Yes,' said the lieutenant. 'There isn't much Will Dayton can't handle. He's one of the toughest men I've ever met.'

But Will Dayton was not feeling so confident as he rode on into the hills. It was already late and he would gain nothing by pushing on through the darkness. He was up against tough and dangerous men too. He didn't want Minty harmed and he knew they would not hesitate to kill her if by doing so they could save their own skins.

Riding again up the ridge top he saw the sun's rim dip down below the horizon. It was time to find camp. The others could not reach the home ranch now and would camp too. He rode on and twilight was an indigo mist on the grassy foothills. He found a suitable spot near a clump of stubby second-growth pines and made his preparations for the night. When he had eaten and fed his horse he was still too restless for sleep. He sat with his back to a tree and watched the stars come out sharp and clear in the blue velvet sky. It was the kind of elemental scene with which over the years and on many a trail he had become familiar. There was a question to bring out, a hard one that demanded an answer. It was the question of the girl and what she had come to mean to him. He remembered now with painful vividness the moment in the hotel bar-room when he had been talking to Belle Macquart and the look in Minty Toween's eyes. It was not the sort of look a man made any mistake about. And now that he knew what it was, he knew too what he felt for her and wondered dismally if he would be too late. Somewhere out in the hills a lone coyote howled to its mate and the cry drove him to his blanket and the long hours of restless sleep on the cold ground.

He woke early and after a small breakfast he rode on over towards the Toller ranch. It was situated at the base of a steep cliff in a kind of cup formed by the folding of the hills and he reached the rocky eastern lip in the early afternoon. For a time he sat his horse, staring down at the distant huddle of shacks and corrals. His sun-darkened face was still and unmoving, giving no hint of the wicked flame within him. Finally he put spurs to the bay and rode straight down towards the ranchhouse across the wide tawny acres of the Toller range.

As he rode past the first corral he was aware of every shape and movement in the vicinity. But the shapes were only trees or a bunkhouse over to his left, two horses, a roan and a buckskin, in a small enclosure. No sign of life. Something was wrong. There should be some activity round a big ranch-house at this time of day.

He rode into the yard and dismounted at the steps of the house. He flung the bay's reins round a rail and slowly went up the steps. He knocked twice on the door and heard a deep voice within say raspingly, 'Come in.'

The door opened easily to his thrusting hand but once inside he could see very little with eyes accustomed to the bright sunlight. A voice said, 'I'm over here, stranger. Give it a minute and you'll see me.'

Slowly Dayton's eyes picked out the details of the darkened room, a wide fireplace and beyond it the figure of a man in a rocker, blanket wrapped around the knees. Dayton came forward and stood on the hearth.

'What are you after, mister?' said the rasping voice.

'I want the girl,' said Dayton. 'Hand her over now and there'll be no more trouble.'

The man in the chair chuckled briefly. 'What girl, mister?'

'It's Minty Toween I'm speaking of,' said Dayton. 'Hand her over or I'll tear this place apart.'

'You're Will Dayton, ain't you? I'm Mark Toller.' He said it as if there was an answer there to all that Dayton had asked.

'I ought to know,' said Dayton. 'We had a fight over the spurline. It doesn't signify now. I want the girl.'

'There's no girl here,' said Toller. He

sounded tired, dispirited, truthful.

'Where is she?'

Toller made no reply and Dayton moved suddenly and swiftly across the hearth reaching for the figure in the chair. He heaved Toller to his feet and found himself staring into the sightless eyes of a blind man. Slowly he eased Mark Toller back into his chair.

'I didn't know,' he said.

'Yes, I'm blind,' said Toller. 'Been blind more than a year now.' Slowly Dayton brought himself back to his mission.

'Two of your men abducted the girl night before last on the trail out of Warbonnet. I aim to take the girl back. Back home. She can pay off the money her grandfather owed, you know.'

'She ain't here, Dayton. My son, Brad, runs things around here now and he don't say much to me any more.'

'If he isn't here, then where do I find him?'

The old man did not answer him. Instead he said almost as if to himself, 'So he's sunk as low as kidnapping now.'

'A man can't sink much lower,' said Dayton.

'No,' said Toller. 'No. That's true enough.' He paused and then said almost as if the words were wrenched from him. 'There's only two places where he could be. One's the line cabin on the upper pasture. The other's Nugget.'

He paused as if appalled at what he had said.

'And now get out,' he blazed. 'You'll get no more of me. No one in this goddam world's goin' to git any more out of me.'

Dayton turned away and went out without speaking. He crossed the porch and down the steps to the tired horse waiting for him. Some of the tension now had drained out of him and he stood there momentarily in the soft late afternoon sunlight almost too weary to climb into the saddle. At last he mounted and rode out. He headed now north-west of the Toller place and soon he began to move up-grade into hill country across the wide spaces of grazing land. The sudden realisation of Toller's blindness had been a shock. The man he had been speaking to was no more than a shadow, a ghost.

The sun dipped down below the distant mountains and blue light flowed gently across the landscape. It took him two hours of steady riding to reach the high tableland where he knew the Toller line camp was. It was full dark when he got there but the rising moon was strong enough to show him the cabin and its clump of protective pines.

He approached warily but could see no smoke rising, no light showing. Slowly he dismounted when he was about a hundred and fifty yards from the cabin. He left the bay with reins trailing. His hand crept down to his holstered gun and tested it. It was loose and ready. He approached the cabin from the rear, every sense alert for trouble. The cabin window was just ahead of him but it revealed nothing, its shutters closed. He cat-footed his way to the front, pausing at the angle of the two walls. And then his whole body seemed to chill into absolute motionless. Someone in the shack had given a low moaning cry.

It was a strange flesh-creeping sound and he waited for it again and pinned it down this time to the crying of a man in great pain. Slowly he edged round the corner of the shack towards the door, drawing his Colts as he moved. He moved swiftly across to the left side of it and then drew back his right leg and kicked it open. There was no response from inside, no light, nothing. And then again the low crying voice, a babble of words and then silence. Dayton thought no one could act that well. With his gun held in front of his stomach he ran in and jumped sideways into the darkness of the wall. There was no gunfire, no movement of any kind, only once more the faint moaning from somewhere in the dark room.

Dayton felt for his matches, struck one and held it high. At first he could make out little and then in the brief strengthening light he saw the man lying on the floor over to his right. He crossed the room, bent down and lit another match. He was looking down at the white pain-racked face of Jed Moss. The front of the man's shirt was a huge dark stain, on his lips a red froth told its terrible tale. He found an oil lamp on a shelf, lit it and then ran out to his horse, grabbed his canteen from the saddle-horn and went back. Very gently he propped the dying man up and tried to make him drink. He succeeded in getting a little water between the slack lips and then suddenly the man's eyes opened.

'How did it happen?' said Dayton.

For a moment he thought it was too late. The man's eyes closed. Again the bloody froth appeared on his lips. Dayton wiped them with his bandanna. The eyes opened again and then slowly Moss began to whisper.

'A gir … a girl,' he said. Dayton bent lower. 'Toller took. Nugget. He … He hit…' His voice rose. 'God damn his dirty son-of-a-bitching soul to hell.' The effort was his last. His eyes rolled back, blood poured once more from his mouth and then he went loose, slack, dead in Dayton's arms.

Dayton got up. He wiped his hands slowly across his mouth as if trying to obliterate something distasteful. There wasn't much doubt about how Jed Moss had died. Trying to stop Brad Toller, most like. Still looking down he thought it was a violent land with too many violent men in it. There should be more for a man to look forward to than this. He made his way out of the shack to his horse. There was a kind of pattern, he thought as he mounted, and from its iron chains it was not possible to escape.

He headed the tired bay up through the trees towards the Pass where the ghost town of Nugget lay. A terrible sense of urgency rode with him now but he dared ask no more of the horse. It had done more than its share of work and now had strength enough only to trot slowly through the shadowy moonlit range. It took him all of two hours to cover the ground to Nugget. At times he rode through trees with the faint light of the stars above him and wind slowly increased its gentle pressure. He was aware of the great fatigue bone-deep in his body, of his empty belly, but most of all of a burning desire to get to Nugget and have done with it all.

He reached the few remaining houses of the former mining-settlement soon after midnight. It stood on a broad shelf just below the main workings that had petered out four years back. A few shacks now, a saloon, the gaunt remains of the old mine-workings. It was and had been for some time a refuge for men on the dodge, badlanders, for men who expected to ride in and out, no questions asked. Dan Maintree who kept the saloon going asked no questions. As Dayton knew, he didn't have to.

Dayton tethered the bay just inside the shelter of the tall pines that came down close to the weathered shacks. He waited there for several minutes getting himself used to the special quality of the place, focussing his attention strictly on the larger bulk of the Acme Saloon. From one shattered window a thin pencil of yellow light pierced the surrounding darkness. They would be there or nowhere, he thought and began to walk quietly along the road towards the buildings. He reached the first doorless and windowless cabin easily and now was within fifty yards of the saloon. A horse whinnied suddenly and Dayton's hand went to his gun-belt. He could see the outlines of places ever more clearly now and drawing near to the shadow-surrounded saloon he saw the horses tethered to the tie rail. There were as far as he could make out four-five of them and they were moving restlessly as if aware of him. He came round a mound of earth and up to the wall of the saloon. He put his right ear against it and could hear a voice, hard and rasping. He could not make out what was said. And then suddenly there was a cry, the cry of a girl in sudden pain. Dayton moved quickly to the front of the saloon, drawing his gun. There was no time now for tactics. He moved straight through the swing doors raising his gun as he went.

CHAPTER THIRTEEN

Riding up from the cabin where Jed Moss lay dead, through the start-hung darkness of the high hills, Minty Toween felt that she had reached the lowest depths of despair. Her pony stumbled wearily after the big black stallion on which rode Brad Toller. Occasionally he gave the lead-rope a vicious tug, as if to remind her of her captivity. They rode on interminably through a pine forest in which the night wind sighed drearily. It was the end she thought hopelessly the end of all her dreams and hopes. For even if Will Dayton managed to trail her to the line-cabin he wouldn't know where they were headed now. She had guessed where it would be. The abandoned mining-settlement called Nugget. She had never been there but had heard that it was the haunt of drifters and outlaws. They plodded on in complete silence broken only by the creak of leather or the jingle of harness, with no word from Brad Toller ahead or from the man called Cal who rode close up behind her. It was all a nightmare and she began to ponder on how to end it. A gun was the answer, was always the answer to the problems of life on the frontier. She would have to wait until they got to their destination and then she would take the first chance that offered. Men didn't readily link up women and guns. She would wait until a holstered gun was in grabbing distance and then...

'We're there,' said Brad Toller.

Minty was just aware of the huddle of buildings ahead of her, deep-shadowed in the moonlight. And then they stopped outside the largest of them. Over her head a big hanging sign creaked faintly in the night wind.

'Trail's end,' said Brad Toller, who had dismounted and was looping his horse's reins around the tie-rail. ''Light, Miss Toween an' come see the nice little surprise I've gotten you.'

She climbed stiffly out of the saddle. As her feet touched ground his right hand hooked itself firmly round her left wrist and holding her like this he led the way into the building. His gun was well out of her reach.

The saloon inside was lit with two kerosene lamps hanging on the wall above a long bar. There were two tables at the far end of the room. A man sat or rather half-lay across the top of the one nearest the bar with his right arm round a whisky bottle. He did not move. One man sat at the second table idly spinning a Colt round his index finger. Two other men stood at the bar, watching the newcomers enter. Hands from the Toller ranch, she guessed.

Still holding her wrist Brad Toller said, 'You've done what I asked?'

'That's your preacher,' said the nearest man at the bar, jerking a thumb in the direction of the man lying across the table.

'He's soaked up the best part of two bottles of whisky,' said the barman sourly. 'At your expense, Mr Toller.'

As if he had not heard, Brad Toller pulled her across the room to where the man lay, snoring, as she could now hear.

'Why, in hell did you let the goddamned fool drink himself stiff?' Toller flared at them.

'Couldn't stop him, Brad,' said the man with the Colt. 'He jes' set at that table when we brung him in an' said as how it was a mortal sin to join anyone in matrimony and that he proposed to drown the thought of it in whisky. That was two hours back.'

'Bring him out of it,' said Toller. 'Throw a

bucket of water over him. Sober him up. There's no time to waste.'

Two of the men standing at the bar advanced on the inert figure of the preacher. They pulled him to his feet and had to struggle to keep him there. Minty saw now that he was tall and bearded. He was wearing a long black coat. She recognised him. He had once ridden by the Toween ranch and had roughly refused Grandpaw Toween's offer of rest and refreshment.

Another man came in now with a wooden bucket of water. The others held the preacher and then the water was thrown full in his face. It brought him out of his drunken stupor and he stood there swaying for a moment or two, with the water dripping down from his hair and beard. His eyes were bewildered and then slowly some sort of recognition came into them. And then this too faded and a wide-eyed stare of blazing fanaticism took its place.

'What am I doing in this god-forsaken place?' he demanded, glaring round at all of them.

'As of now you ain't doin't anything,' snapped Brad Toller. 'But just as soon as you've shaken some of the whisky fumes out of that head of yours, you're goin' to be marryin' me and this' – he glanced briefly down at Minty – 'this lady here.'

'You cannot force a man of God to do anything that he feels is wrong,' said the preacher and Minty's heart leaped within her, reaching out to one faint ray of hope in the man's words.

'You'll do what I say,' said Toller. 'Burn off some of those whiskers, Finn,' he said. 'Just to show the reverend that I mean business.'

The man addressed as Finn holstered the gun he'd been spinning, got out his chair and produced a box of matches from his vest pocket. A grin of sadistic pleasure creased his small mean face.

'Hold him, boys,' he said and struck a match.

The other Toller hands grabbed the preacher again and Finn advanced with the lighted match. He thrust it suddenly towards the man's beard.

'I'll do it. I'll do it,' yelled the preacher. Finn dropped the match and trod on it. 'Right,' said Brad Toller. 'No more tricks or next time I'll have them burn you alive, you goddam old fraud.'

'I am a minister of God,' said the preacher almost to himself. 'But I am a mortal man and I know mortal fear. I will do what you want me to do but under protest.' He sat down mumbling incoherently to himself.

'That's fine,' said Brad Toller and he turned to Minty. He seemed to become aware for the first time of the box she had clung to so long. 'What's in that box?'

'It's a dress,' she said.

'Now that's fine too,' said Toller. 'I never did figure on getting' hitched to a woman in pants. Put it on.'

She felt something shrink within her. The thought of the dress and all it had meant and the long way it had come and only now for this – the last degradation – all of it screamed in her hand now and standing there on the dirty saloon floor she wondered if she was going mad.

'Put it on and make it fast,' said Brad Toller. He laughed. 'No call to get all flustered about taking your clothes off here.'

'Not here,' she breathed.

'There's a pantry in back of the bar,' interposed the barman hurriedly. 'She can use that.'

'Any window or way out?' said Toller.

'It's no more than a cupboard,' said the barman.

'Show her the way.'

Almost before Minty had got round the

back of the bar she heard Toller call out, 'The drinks are on me. Set 'em up, barman.'

The cupboard was small but she managed with trembling fingers to get the string untied and the dress out. An oil lamp burned on a shelf and before putting on the dress, she looked hurriedly round for a gun, knowing even as she looked that it was no more than a store for odds and ends – packets of candles, bottles of whisky, some tins of tomatoes, a big coil of rope. She got the dress on with difficulty, hearing the laughter of the men drinking at the bar, afraid now only of violence and empty of hope now that the final degradation was so near. Hurriedly she rolled up the trouser legs of her old levis. Without realising what she was doing she looked round for a mirror and then half-laughed, half-sobbed at the bitter irony of the thought.

She came out then behind the bar and suddenly the laughter stopped. There was a long strange silence but she was aware of only one thing. Underneath the bartop on a shelf a long black Colts was lying. The men were standing a little further along the bar. They were all staring at her. She took a step forward, pretended to stumble against the bar and the Colts was in her hands. She drew back quickly, the gun rising in her small right hand. She held it on Brad Toller, trying with all her might to keep her hand from shaking.

'I'm goin' out of here,' she said. 'If you try to stop me I'll kill you.'

She looked at the barman who stood no more than six paces away from her.

'Go round the bar and join the others,' she said and the Colts wavered slightly in his direction. The bartender did as he was told. Minty began to edge slowly along the passage behind the bar. Somewhere behind her the preacher said, 'They that take the sword shall perish by the sword.'

'Back up,' she said as she drew near the immobile group. They edged slowly away from the bar and she quickened her step until she reached the end of it. She was only a few steps away from and moving towards the batwing doors of the saloon entrance.

And then Brad Toller laughed.

He said, 'Jest take it away from her, Dan,' and almost at once the big hand reached over as he turned and closed down on the gun in her hand. She fought like a wild cat but the newcomer took the gun off her as if he were taking a toy from a child. And then she was standing there alone, shaking and defeated.

213

Toller said harshly, 'Bring her over here and get that tin-horn preacher on his feet.'

She was pushed roughly towards the bar and someone nudged the preacher in her direction. Brad Toller stood by her side.

'I do this under protest,' said the preacher.

'Jest git the marryin' over an' done with, preacher. You can do all the protestin' you want afterwards,' said Toller.

She heard the jumble of words coming from the man in black. She felt Toller's hand close like a vice on her upper arm. She stared at it, seeing for the first time that the wrist wore a thin black circlet.

'Answer,' said Toller.

'No,' she screamed. 'No,' and then she felt the grip relax and she heard a voice say, 'Stand away from them, Minty,' and she began to weep, the tears of happiness suddenly streaming down her cheeks.

Will Dayton stood there for a breathing space waiting for her to move and then he saw one man's hand twitch and blur to his gun-butt. Dayton drew and fired. His bullet hit the Toller hand at the base of the throat. He went over as if a giant hand had struck him down. And then the two lights above the bar were suddenly extinguished. There was nothing now but the warm smoke-

214

scented darkness, a man breathing heavily, the scuff of a boot along the plank floor. Bent low, Dayton moved now with Indian soft-footedness away and around to the far side of the room. A gun opened up and roared twice. In the swift bloom and flash from the gun-muzzle he could see the three men but not the girl. He raised his gun and fired again. There was a high cry of agony and the heavy thud of a body striking the floor. A Toller gun roared again and a bullet hit the wall behind him. He said, moving as he spoke: 'You'd better chuck in your hand. I'll kill you all if you don't.'

The only reply was a blast of gunfire that achieved nothing more than the shattering of a window. And then a voice unknown to Dayton yelled: 'Count me out. Count me out.' And there was a sudden pounding of feet and a body hurtled through the bat-wings and then silence again broken only by the diminished swaying of the half-doors.

One less, he thought and moving again found himself touching the far end of the long bar. There would still be three men. Brad Toller, one of his hands and the man who had been about to marry them. Dayton bent low and inched his way along the inside of the bar, listening. He heard it then, the very faintest noise ahead of him, between the bar itself and the wall. It could be Minty, he realised and there was only one way in which to be sure. He could strike a light and fire if need be. The chances were now fully against him. He reached with his left hand into his vest pocket. Took out his match-box and still using only the fingers of his left hand, withdrew a match. He would have to use his thumbnail and keep the light well away from his own body. With his gun ready he extended his left hand and snicked the match alight. A gun roared not seven yards from him and he fired back twice at the flashes. There was a strangled and terrible cry of pain and then silence. Dayton waited.

'Brad?' said a voice high and tense. 'You O.K Brad?'

'He won't answer because he can't,' said Dayton. 'He's dead.'

'If I throw down my guns an' walk on out,' said the voice, 'will you shoot me in the back or let me go on walkin'?'

'Throw down your guns,' said Dayton. 'But don't try walking out. Get round to the back of the bar and light a lamp.'

There were two quick, heavy thuds as the man's guns hit the floor. Dayton heard his footsteps as he came round to the back of the bar, heard him pause and withdraw a box of matches from wherever he kept them. Then there was the blue spurt of a match, and a hand reached up to the kerosene lamp hanging above the bar. And then two guns flashed and roared almost simultaneously. One was over to Dayton's left, the second came from the man near the lamp. He had managed to light the lamp and fire almost in the same movement but too late. The bullet hit him full in the chest and he slumped down to the floor.

Looking around in the lamplight Dayton saw Minty Toween standing way back from the bar, a gun still smoking in her hand.

'I figure that just about evens things between us, Minty,' he said quietly.

'Will,' she said, 'Will, I didn't think you would come. It was when he said, "You O.K Brad." You see, it was Brad Toller's voice. So I watched and waited. There was a gun on the floor and I used that, when his hand came up and I saw that black band on his wrist. I fired then.'

She was trembling now with exhaustion and hysteria. 'I didn't think you'd come,' she said.

He stood there looking at her in the faint smoke-hung light of the bar-room and knew at last what she meant to him.

'I was coming,' he said gently. 'Kinda slowly maybe but I got here.' He came round the bar to where she still stood and took the gun out of her hand.

'We'll have to ride down and tell the Marshal about all this,' he said.

'Of course,' she said, quietly. 'I'll have to get back to the ranch then.'

'I was figuring on something else,' he said.

'Kindly don't tell me that a woman ain't capable of running a ranch by herself,' she said with a return to her former temper.

'No,' he said slowly. 'No. I've got a piece of land over the border in Idaho territory. I was wonderin' whether you'd consider...?' He tailed off suddenly, embarrassed. Suddenly aware too of the great gulf of years between them.

'Are you tryin' to propose to me, Will Dayton?' she said. 'Because if so I accept. I'll marry you with real pleasure.'

'Yes,' he said. 'Yes, ma'am. I reckon you could call it a proposal,' and without more ado he took her in his arms and kissed her.

'Reckon Idaho'll suit me fine,' she said at last a little breathlessly.

'I was thinking it might be a whole lot easier for me to keep an eye on you if I'm married to you than to have to ride the whole frontier every time you're in trouble.'

They both heard the scrabbling noise coming from the far corner of the room and both watched the tall ungainly figure lurch towards them. The barman also emerged from his cupboard behind the bar.

'If I'm not mistaken,' said the preacher. 'I was about to perform a wedding ceremony.'

Dayton looked down at Minty with a question in his eyes.

'Yes,' she said. 'Oh! Yes.'

'You can't be married without a witness,' said the preacher.

Dayton turned to the barman.

'Will you stand up for me?' he said.

'Yes,' said the barman. 'It'll be a real pleasure.'

And so they were married a long time ago in the tumbledown bar-room of a hotel that's long forgotten now in a ghost town that's blown away in the winds of time. But in Idaho they still remember the Daytons and how they ran their cattle and raised a big family and how Grandma Dayton was known from time to time to tell her grandchildren some pretty tall stories about what went on in the old frontier days.

This Large Print Book, for people
who cannot read normal print,
is published under the auspices of

THE ULVERSCROFT FOUNDATION